I0575812

THE DIVINE ARCHIVE #0

FLOODWATERS

WREN L. RIVERS

Copyright © 2025 Wren L. Rivers
First Edition, 2025

All rights reserved.

No part of this publication may be reproduced, distributed, or transmitted in any form or by any means, including photocopying, recording, or other electronic or mechanical methods, without the prior written permission of the publisher.

NO AI TRAINING: Any use of this publication to "train" generative artificial intelligence (AI) technologies to generate text is expressly prohibited.

Cover Illustration by Wren L. Rivers

Developmental Editing by Nicole Evans @ Thoughts Stained Editorial

ISBN 979-8-9931437-0-5 (eBook)

ISBN 979-8-9931437-2-9 (Paperback)

Library of Congress Control Number: 2025921420

The story, all names, characters, and incidents portrayed in this production are fictitious. No identification with actual persons (living or deceased), places, buildings, and products is intended or should be inferred. No generative AI was used in the creation of this book.

CONTENT WARNING

This story contains content that may be unsettling to some readers, including graphic violence, major character death, suicide, murder, child death, drowning, gun violence, and religious themes.

1

43rd Dew, Prosperity 2192

Later designated as the year Great Flood 01

One thousand years before *Blood of the Gods*

Some people died loudly. Others, with nothing more than a whisper.

A soldier under heavy gunfire, screaming in agony as blood gushed from her wounds. An elderly man, asleep on his deathbed, slipping into oblivion the moment his visitors stepped out for coffee. Either way, the human body shut down one organ at a time, until it realized there was nothing left to keep alive.

But was there any death more torturous than that of a group science project? Eris didn't think so.

He sat draped over the old living room couch, its upholstery worn and matted from far too many years of use, and twirled a blue ballpoint pen between his fingers. He had long since looked away from the notebook balanced on his lap, his gaze trailing lazily around the room. Was there *anything* more interesting than his homework? It seemed not. His gaze met nothing but woven prayer mats and bland, undecorated walls. He threw his head back over the arm of the couch, catching a glimpse of his companion.

Miri Chase was a quiet girl with a bob of brown hair, which curled toward her face like a round, decorative frame. She was a sophomore, though by some manner of happenstance, she'd wound up in junior-level classes. Eris never once considered her, and he would have preferred to continue that streak, if not for Mr. Darren, who had paired them for the final research project of the year.

On the first day they worked together, she had looked him up and down, eyeing his mussed blond hair and grass-stained tee shirt, then said, *"I can do the whole thing, if you want."*

"What?"

"I know your type," she elaborated. *"Jocks. You usually make me do all the work."*

"Oh. No, I'm not like that."

Now, Miri met his gaze and adjusted her round glasses, her earnest face upside-down from his perspective. She sat cross-legged on the beige loveseat perpendicular to Eris's couch, holding a library book in her hands. Its pages were stained and creased. "What's wrong?"

"Sue me, but *Tree Biodiversity's Impact on Local Squirrel Populations* isn't the most exhilarating paper we could be writing."

"That's what we proposed, though. We can't change it now. Mr. Darren said if the subject isn't what we proposed, he'll dock us a letter grade. Remember?"

"I know," Eris groaned, drawing out the *o*. "Want to take a break, at least? My mom n' dad will be home soon. They're picking Aria up from soccer practice. Ugh, she's so annoying. We'll want to be out of the house."

"Where would we go? Do you have your license?"

"Not yet. We can walk somewhere, though. I'm antsy to move my legs."

"Sure."

Eris led Miri to the foyer and toed his sneakers on. As he waited for Miri to zip on her ankle-high boots, he nabbed his inhaler off the console table and tucked it into his pocket. He opened the front door, and as soon as Miri was ready, he ushered her out into the temperate dew season air.

A yellow car pulled into the tiny urban driveway. Its grumbling engine cut short, and out climbed Mom and Dad, a screaming Aria in tow. Eris marched past them, Miri following in his wake. If he was fast enough, he could escape before his parents forced him into daycare duty. He called over his shoulder, "We're going for a walk!"

Mom and Dad did not stop him. They were too preoccupied with Aria, who stomped her foot on the asphalt and wailed.

"Poor girl," Miri cooed. "Not easy being six, huh?"

"I wish she would shut up." Eris kicked a rock down the sidewalk. "She hates sports. But she doesn't realize how easy she's got it. Mom 'n Dad switch it up yearly. They're trying to find something she'll like. They forced *me* to play basketball 'till I was thirteen. It took a huge argument to convince them to let me play lacrosse."

"I can't do sports. I'm not built for it. Fine by me, though. I think they're boring." Miri paused. "Dad makes me take piano lessons, though, so I get it. He insists it's a good skill to have, but I don't really like the instrument."

Eris couldn't fathom the concept of a sport being boring, but he said nothing. He kicked the rock again, and it clattered a few paces ahead. They settled into an uneasy silence. Should he try to keep the conversation going? What were they supposed to talk about, aside from their project?

Miri must have been thinking the same thing.

"Swathi says there's a god visiting Midir," she said. "Swathi's a friend of mine. We sit next to each other in Advanced Literature."

"A god?" Eris repeated, casting Miri a sideways glance. "Which one?"

"I don't know. She told me she saw him, though. Dressed in flowy robes. Too pristine and ethereal to be human. I mean, I guess it's always possible she'd just seen some random guy, but she seemed rather set on it."

"May he grace us with kindness," Eris muttered. A half-prayer. There was no way to pray in earnest without knowing which god one prayed to. Prayers to nobody went nowhere. But, as Mom and Dad always insisted, the act of faith was most important.

"I wonder if I'll ever get to see him. Wouldn't that be cool? To meet a god?"

"Anesh is a huge city. He could be anywhere. Heck, he could be anywhere in *Midir.*"

Miri took Eris by the wrist and hurried down the sidewalk. Eris had half a heart to wrench his hand away, for fear of someone seeing, but he didn't. They weaved through alleyways, past Wayfarer High School, and through the business district. When they skidded to a halt in the town square, both teenagers were panting for breath. Sweat dampened Eris's hair, slicking choppy blond tufts to his forehead.

He took a puff from his inhaler, held his breath for a few seconds, then exhaled.

"Swathi said she saw him down that street," Miri said. "He might still be in the area. He could be staying in a hotel nearby."

"A hotel? I doubt a god would be staying in a *hotel.*"

"Well, do you have any better ideas?"

"Do you think..." Eris spoke slowly, with trepidation, as he and Miri approached the grand fountain in the center of the square. He sat on the fountain's lip, eager to rest his legs. Water misted the back of his neck.

Miri scanned the ledge, then sat a shoulder's distance away, far enough to avoid the brown-white splotch of bird poop next to Eris's thigh. "Do I think what?"

"Do you think, if we met the god, we could change our thesis?"

"Isn't a scientific paper about the divine a bit contradictory?"

"Well, sure. But we don't have to write about theology. Hear me out: *The Effect of Divine Presence on Human Behavior.* It's not about the god, per se. It's more about the response."

Miri grinned. "Better than squirrel populations, hm?"

"Much better."

"Let's do it." She held out her hand as though a high school paper was a business deal. "I'll take the lowered grade, but we *have* to blow Mr. Darren out of the water."

Eris shook on it. Miri's grip was firmer than he had anticipated.

"Our control group?" Miri asked.

"Churchgoers?"

"Hm. I think we should have three levels. Control group could be atheists. *Then* we have churchgoers—the first stage of divine presence. Spiritual presence. Right? And then, above that, we study folks who have interacted with the god."

"Good thinking."

"And if we fail, well..." Miri snickered. "We always have the squirrels."

Eris stood. "Let's get searching."

They combed the streets until the sun was low. At twilight, after a whole lot of nothing, Miri called for Eris to stop. She stood on the sidewalk, hands on her knees. "My legs hurt," she complained. "And I'm hungry. Let's call it a night."

Streetlights flicked on. Eris propped his foot against the curb and stretched his calves. "Do you think your parents could come pick us up?"

"I'll call them. Hang on."

Miri stepped a few paces away and held her phone to her ear. Eris allowed her some privacy. He wandered down the sidewalk, kicking his feet out in front of him with each languid step. *At the corner,* he thought, *I'll turn around and come back.*

But when he reached the corner, he paused.

On Compton Street, there stood a derelict warehouse. He knew it well. When he was fourteen, he and his teammates would sneak in after practice to explore. Its vast, empty room was the perfect space for them to get the remainder of their energy out.

He'd scrawled a rather crude, inappropriate picture along the walls in chalk, once. Another time, Marco Peterson dared him to climb all the way to the little circular window at the top. He did, of course, because he wasn't a wuss, but he got stuck up there. The fire department had to help him down.

He hadn't been in the building since. Mom and Dad forbade it. For good reason, he supposed, with the unidentifiable plants that crawled their way up crumbling walls. Grimy signs warned passersby that the warehouse was condemned, their lettering faded, scratched, graffitied.

A little girl, Aria's age, played with a red ball half her size. Her father lingered nearby, phone in his hand, his forehead wrinkled from the strain of his furrowed brow. Down the block, a passerby walked, making his way somewhere important, if his brisk pace was any indicator. A quiet evening, tonight. Rare in a city like Anesh.

The girl tossed the ball into the air. She fumbled her catch, and the ball rolled across the road, bumping the curb in front of the warehouse. The girl looked left, right, then left again—diligent, well-taught—and hurried across to fetch her toy.

"...come pick us up?" Miri's voice floated into his ears. *"Oh, right, I forgot you said you were working late tonight... We were doing some research for our paper... Me 'n Eris. My classmate. No, you haven't met him. Yeah, he's nice."*

A creak. A groan. The wood was too termite-eaten to hold out any longer, and once-shiny steel was browned with rust and decay. Supports gave way. Something along the far side of the warehouse toppled with a cacophonous crash. The girl's father looked up from his phone in alarm.

"Hey!" Eris yelled to the girl, waving, beckoning her. "Get out of there!"

The girl's feet remained rooted to the pavement beneath her. She stared up at the warehouse, trembling. Her father stepped off the curb with little regard for his own safety, intent on rushing to grab her.

He did not make it far. Something deep within the warehouse snapped, and the building collapsed.

A thick wave of dust and debris flooded the street. Eris covered his mouth with his sleeve to filter out the sour air, though the gesture did him little good. His lungs ached. His eyes watered. Still, he squinted through the thick dust cloud—somewhere beneath it all, was that girl a bloodied, crushed corpse?

Miri rushed to his side, phone still pressed to her ear. She surveyed the wreckage, her green eyes wet thanks to the dirt lingering in the air. "Oh, *Heavens*. Dad, I-I gotta go. We'll walk home. See you later."

Eris caught Miri's dad's frantic '*are you okay?*' over the phone's tinny speaker moments before she cut the call.

The dust settled, and hunched in the street stood the girl, cuts littering her skin. A man stood over her, his long black hair descending upon her like a veil. He'd blocked her from the brunt of the collapse, and somehow, he too was alive. How?

Blood dripped from a wound at the man's temple, trailing its way down his cheekbones. The blood wasn't crimson, but rather a shimmering gold, which caught the yellow light of the streetlamps above.

"Miri," Eris gasped, taking in the man's draped robes, marred with dust. "Look."

As if she wasn't already looking.

"What happened? I heard the crash, but I was down the street, I didn't see—"

"His blood," was all Eris could get out. "Look, his blood. It's not red."

This was divine blood. There was no other explanation.

Miri coughed into the crook of her arm. She said nothing, but Eris could see the wonder on her face. Her jaw was slack, lips parted enough to show a hint of teeth. She couldn't quite tear her gaze away.

The girl's father rushed to her and scooped her into his arms. Gripping his daughter tight to his chest, he gasped out a long string of what Eris could only presume were reverent thank-yous. He spoke too softly for Eris to hear across the wide street. Eris did, however, catch the daughter's high, elated voice.

"He healed me!" she exclaimed. She held up her arm, caked in crimson and gold, but with no wound in sight. "Look, daddy! He healed me!"

The man rose. He was tall, with broad shoulders and a tan, chiseled face, as though he were carved out of marble. Eris had seen this face before, painted in murals and sculpted on statues; a face borne of seafoam and brine.

He was the God King, Einari.

2

Eris shared science class with his teammate Adrien. Today, Adrien sat in the back corner, leaning his chair back on its hind legs, chewing gum he wasn't allowed to have. Eris usually sat next to him. Not this time.

Mr. Darren had allowed his students a free period, with the expectation that the class spent the hour working on their group projects. The classroom was alight with chatter, the occasional comment about the pH of soap or the frequency of radio waves breaking over the monotonous hum of voices.

Adrien's project partner was Lucas, who did marching band in the autumn and rowing in the spring. Rowing saved him from loser status. He bridged *band nerd* and *jock* just enough to slide through high school undetected by the social elite. Eris couldn't remember what instrument Lucas played. Maybe the tuba.

"The fact that it's Einari complicates things," Miri was saying. Tired of pushing her hair out of her face, she rifled through her backpack until she found a yellow barrette, which she clipped into place above her temple. "I mean, I might be overthinking it. But people are going to react differently to the God King's presence than they would to any lesser god."

"Well, we can't exactly ask another god to come visit."

Miri laughed. "Yeah."

A ball of wadded-up paper hit the back of Eris's head and tumbled to the floor.

"Miri and Eris, sitting in a tree," Adrien jeered from across the room. Lucas snickered. *"K-I-S-S-I-N-G."*

Eris knew a reaction, positive or negative, would only further fuel the fire. He ignored Adrien. Mr. Darren held a different opinion, however. From his desk at the front of the classroom, he snapped, "Adrien, get to work. And spit that gum out."

His attempt was valiant but unsuccessful. Adrien ripped another blank sheet from his notebook, crumpled it, and lobbed it across the room.

Miri was a good sport. If Adrien and Lucas bothered her, she didn't show it. Instead, she passed Eris her phone, a bold, declarative headline on its screen. "I found an article that was published a few days ago. Give this a read."

God King Saves Child's Life

On 43rd Dew, the condemned Gilmore Warehouse collapsed. Ilse Petromi, age five, was playing near the site.

The building, slated for destruction on 13th Sun, was once home to Gilmore Industries, the leading innovators in automotive technology, bankrupt in Prosperity 2103. The warehouse was never purchased by a successor.

"His Grace saved her life. I am his faithful servant. I owe him everything," said Tomás Petromi, Ilse's father.

Ilse Petromi is currently staying at Charity General Hospital. Though uninjured, her clothing was bloodied, leaving doctors vexed. Her diagnosis: shock.

"He healed her wounds," said Tomás. "A few drops of his blood. That's all it took."

Though no scientific conclusion has come of this yet, the question stands: can the substance researchers are now referring to as God's Blood cure wounds?

"Okay," Eris said, sliding Miri's phone back across the lab table. The charms clipped to it jingled. A little acrylic bee and a ladybug. "This is great. I mean, I don't think Mr. D would've accepted our eyewitness account, for fear we'd made it up. But this is reputable."

"Are you free tonight?" Miri asked. "I want to talk to Mr. Petromi."

"I've got lacrosse after school, but I could meet after. We're just doing drills today. I'll be done by five."

"I'll see if I can find his contact info. Meet me at the Sage & Tallow on fifth street at... six-thirty? Is that doable?"

"I'll be there."

Miri tucked her binder, one of the fancy ones with rubber reinforcement along the edges, into her backpack. The bell rang, and she was the first out the door.

Sage & Tallow was a coffee shop, not a butcher like the name seemed to suggest. The name sounded dignified to those who did not know what tallow was, and disgusting to those who did. Must have been intentional. To steer away snooty folk and vegans. The place was locally owned, as opposed to the cheapo chain shop across the street, Golden Hour Coffeehouse, which gained twice as much foot traffic and served half as good drinks.

Eris arrived ten minutes early, ordered himself a caramel latte using money he'd stolen from Mom's wallet, then settled upon a small couch nestled in the back corner and texted Miri. *I'm here.*

While he waited, his eyes wandered. The walls were covered in as many picture frames as could fit, leaving not much more than a thin maze of dark green paint between them. Each frame looked different. Thrifted, most likely. Eclectic.

The same went for the furniture. The couch Eris sat on was light brown, its upholstery stained by spilt coffee. There was not a single other couch like it in the entire shop. The table in front of him was square, but a few paces to his left was a tall, round table surrounded by velvet-padded barstools.

The bell hanging from the door chimed, and in walked Miri. Eris sat up straight and waved. She glanced his way, offered a small smile, then made for the front. She didn't linger there long. She grabbed a mobile order off the counter without exchanging a single word with the barista.

"I found Mr. Petromi's email address during lunch," Miri said as she sank onto the couch beside Eris. "He replied by mid-afternoon. Said he'll meet up with us at seven."

Eris nodded. They had thirty minutes to kill. Not long enough to go out and do anything, too long to sit in awkward silence. Eris sipped on his latte and eyed Miri's. The side of the cup had a printed label on it, which read: *Green Tea—Robert Chase.*

"You could have gotten anything," Eris opted to say. "But you got green tea?"

"Sure," Miri said with a shrug. "Well, Papa was happy to buy me whatever I wanted, but Dad insisted that it couldn't have a ton of caffeine this late. Didn't want me up all night."

"You have two dads?" Eris blurted.

"Yeah? What of it?"

"Nothing, I just... I've never met anyone like that. Do you ever wish you had a mom? Someone you can relate to, or whatever?"

"Not really. Dad and Papa love doing *girl things* with me. Their words, not mine. Papa lets me do makeup on him. He's an engineer for his day job, but he performs drag on the weekends. And Dad takes me to these STEM For Girls conferences twice a year. They're pretty fun."

"You do both?" Eris asked. "Makeup and math?"

"...Yes? They're not mutually exclusive."

"Oh. Cool."

Eris tapped his fingers against his knee. His eyes darted around the room. He stared at a rather ugly painting of a sunset, taking in its blotchy, uneven brushstrokes and its gaudy colors. Not that Eris could do any better, but would it hurt the coffee shop owners to have something a bit nicer to look at?

Right next to it was an illustration of a clown, housed in a round gold frame. Not much better. Still, he supposed, it was better than looking at Miri. Staring at a grinning clown portrait was much less awkward, even if it was a bit unnerving.

"So, we'll interview Mr. Petromi," Miri said, after a while. Eris glanced over at her. She had a notebook out. On it, a checklist. Miri's handwriting was neat. Far neater than Eris's. "He'll be our first source, aside from the article. From there, we could go to a temple and interview a few folks. The only issue, though, is that anyone at a major temple is bound to worship Einari. And now that the news has confirmed his presence, people are going to, by nature, act differently. Our results are going to be skewed by circumstance. I guess we should just lean into it."

"My parents force me to attend a niche temple every week. Nobody there *dislikes* Einari, but it's one of those god-specific ones, for those who are primarily devout to one," Eris said.

"Which god?" Miri asked, tilting her head, interested.

"Ugh. The Fool."

"Oh! I suppose I should have guessed. Your name—"

Eris didn't let her finish her sentence. "I hate my name. Someday, I'm going to be punished for my parents' decision. Once I'm old enough, I'm changing it. Something simple, like John."

"John? You don't strike me as a John."

"Peter?"

"No. Too stuffy."

"Lawrence?"

"Ew!" Miri laughed. She typed something on her phone. "I like Eris. Not that my opinion means much. You gotta do what's most comfortable for you. But I think it's the kind of name that can mean whatever you want it to. Look, see here: *Eris. Origin: Køveni. Derived from Aeris, the god of the sky. People with this name prioritize freedom, vitality, and ambition.* It's not really about *Aeris,* Eris. It's about you."

"I guess."

"Anyway, if you want me to call you John or Peter or Lawrence, I will."

"Maybe someday. Not yet."

The door chimed. A familiar man stood in the entryway, with warm brown skin and graying hair. His eyes skimmed the room. Miri waved, and he approached, his arms folded, nervous.

"Hello, Mr. Petromi!" Miri greeted with a welcoming smile. She gestured toward the empty seat across the table. "Sit down. We won't take too much of your time. Just had a few questions for you, is all. How's your daughter?"

"She's well," he said. He was a softspoken man, though Eris had trouble gauging whether that was the norm, or if he was still shaken by the ordeal. "The hospital discharged her last night, and she was smiling as bright as ever. I feel so horrible. Work has been hectic. Too many business deals to close—if I hadn't been wrapped up in answering messages, I would've stopped her..."

"Glad she's well," Eris said. His paper cup was long since empty, but he feigned taking a sip. He wasn't sure what to do with his hands.

Miri placed her phone in the center of the table, screen up, a recorder app open. "Do you mind if I record our conversation? It'll help us when we write our report."

"That's fine."

Miri tapped the red icon at the bottom of her screen, then sat back. "Can you summarize your experience with Einari and your daughter?"

"Well, like I said, I'd been dealing with some work matters. Ilse is a good kid, most of the time, so I trusted that I could look away from her for a moment. A contractor had been sending angry messages. When the building came down on her, I was terrified. I can't put into words how relieved I was to see her alive. I hadn't seen His Grace coming."

"Can you tell us what your relationship with faith is?" Miri asked.

"I'd always considered myself agnostic. Until—until the collapse, I guess. I swore to him I'd devote everything I had. You're too young to know it, but someday, when you're older, you'll understand. You'll do anything for your children. You'd give your own life for them. I quit my job yesterday. Spent the entire day at the Temple of the God King. The big one by the harbor. Have you ever been? Beautiful cathedral."

Eris shook his head. Mom and Dad only cared about attending one little, near-forgotten temple. He wished he could attend sermons at the Temple of the God King, but the best he could do was bike past it on occasion.

Would he be allowed in if people knew he was named after the Fool? Would the Book of the Tide he stowed under his bed be enough to prove his devotion? Would he have to repent double-time, for the sake of his family?

"Can you describe how it felt?" Eris asked. "To have such a close encounter with a god?"

"Breathtaking," Mr. Petromi said. "And crushing, all at once. I felt so small, so humble. A speck of dust, compared to him. His blood—it glittered under the streetlights. I've never seen blood that color, and I never will again."

"Well, we don't want to keep you," Miri said. "I'm sure you're still a bit rattled. We appreciate you taking your time to help us with our project."

A few pleasantries and goodbyes, then he was gone. A random face in Anesh's crowd of residents. Eris couldn't help but feel bad for thinking of him as a data point.

"I have a program that can turn audio files to text," Miri said. "I'll get you a transcript by tonight. Could you start a rough draft of our introduction?"

"Sure."

"Do you want a ride home? Plenty of room in Papa's car."

"No, thanks." Eris replied. "I've got my bike."

Miri chuckled. "Best get going, then. Before it gets too dark out."

The Temple of the God King was on the opposite side of the district, but Eris took the detour anyhow. He skidded to a halt outside its ornate bronze doors and hitched his bike to the rusted iron rack along the sidewalk. Then, he tugged at his bike lock once, twice. Just to double-check.

Eris approached the temple's doors. He placed his palms against the cool metal surface, its intricate bas relief details—swirling lines and expressive human figures—pressing into the pads of his fingers. He pushed the doors open. They were heavy, but nothing he hadn't expected. The hinges groaned. Thousands of years old, this cathedral must be, kept standing by those who devoted their livelihoods to Einari.

Eris wasn't sure what he felt more awestruck by. The prospect of seeing a god in the flesh? Or this? A cathedral several stories tall, with domed ceilings decorated with vibrant murals? This building was designed to evoke a sense of the divine. *This* was what a proper temple should look like. Aeris's puny temple, which stood sandwiched between industrial buildings, was nothing in comparison. A speck of dust.

Eris sat in the backmost pew, even though the off-hours emptiness meant he could have sat anywhere. His fear of intruding kept him close to the doors, where he could make an easy escape, should he need. His phone buzzed in his pocket. A brief glance revealed a text message from Mom. *Will you be home soon? Dinner's almost ready.*

I'm on my way, Eris texted back. *Got caught up with school project stuff after practice.*

He tucked his phone away and folded his hands together.

"Dearest king," he muttered under his breath. "Please, forgive me for how I am named. Forgive me for my family's faith. Those are outside of my control. I can't stay in your temple long, but let it be known. I believe Aeris takes up precious space among the Big Four and offers little for it."

A moment passed. Even a breath felt loud enough to echo through the cathedral.

"I hold tight to my faith," Eris recited. A prayer from the Book of the Tide he'd memorized. *"As the tides ebb and flow, His Grace remains constant, and so too shall I."*

He sat for a few minutes longer, then rode home.

The Effect of Divine Presence on Human Behavior

By Eris Vandermere and Miri Chase

It's no secret that the gods have an impact on mortal behavior. From the beginning of time, the ~~citizens~~ denizens(?) of Midir worshipped a pantheon of gods, starting from the Big Four and eventually growing to include a lot of smaller gods, too. There's a lot of arguments about whether the gods existed before humans or if human belief is what created the gods. The Theological Journal states in its Prosperity 2060 essay, The Beginning of Humankind: "The gods created us. There is no reason to believe that we created gods. We simply discovered them." (Norris, 5).

On an otherwise pretty normal day this year, a god showed up. This was witnessed by ~~us~~—Eris Vandermere and Miri Chase. The Anesh Gazette reported on a collapsed warehouse that nearly killed a five-year-old girl, Ilse Petromi. But the God King Einari saved her and cured her wounds. Vandermere and Chase witnessed a shift of faith that day. Tomás Petromi, Ilse's dad, was once agnostic, but upon meeting His Grace, he knelt before Einari and swore a renewed faith.

The presence of a god changes people in a fundamental way. In this essay, we will track Einari's travels through Anesh and study how he affects the behavior of people he meets.

Eris sat back and stretched his arms above his head, turning his gaze away from his computer. Sunlight peeked through his blinds and landed in long stripes across the floor. He'd been up since before sunrise, eager to have *something* to show Miri today. He would need to get ready for school soon. He had an hour until the bus was scheduled to come, though, so he went for a jog.

His favorite aspect of city jogging was the freedom to go as far as he wanted. He was not constrained to the length of any one trail, like in the suburbs where he was born. Anesh's infrastructure consisted of a neat, straight grid, and most street crossings boasted those flashy yellow lights that warned drivers of pedestrians. He could run to the city limits, or he could turn around anywhere in the interim. He could turn any corner and run any block, and every road could lead him back home.

While the possibilities were endless, he did have a preferred jogging route, which took him across the bridge to Southside. He didn't visit Southside in any other instance than to run, as its bright murals and weird-looking architecture kept him stimulated.

He paused to catch his breath on a street corner whose lights were yet to turn off, despite the morning sun casting long stripes of light across the streets. His chest ached and his breaths came in wheezes. He took a puff from his inhaler.

This unremarkable street corner seemed as good a place as any to turn around. He cast a glance at his watch. The timer on its tiny screen read fifteen minutes. Perfect. Plenty of time to get home, shower, and catch the bus. He turned and started his jog back home. Through Southside, across the bridge...

At the end of the bridge, crossing back from Southside to the Central Quarter, Eris heard a ragged, desperate voice. Gritting his teeth, he kept his attention pinned ahead of him. *Don't come begging to me,* he thought. *I don't have any money.* He jogged at a quicker pace and wished he'd brought his headphones.

"Please, sir," the voice floated up from somewhere below the bridge. "A drop of blood, Your Grace, that's all I need, just a drop... My father is dying. You could help him. Please. I'll do anything."

Eris dug his heels into the pavement and ground to a halt. He dared to peer over the bridge's rim. On the narrow strip of shore before the river, a beggar knelt. The God King stood over them. Einari had his hair pulled into a bun today, kept away from his face. Most artists depicted his hair as a waterfall, spraying mist and foam at his shoulders. Now, bound to the constraints of a mortal body, it took on a shiny black hue, with strands so thin that a few chunks refused to stay confined by his hair tie. Some had slipped from the thick blue band and fell in front of his ear, ghosting against his sharp, sun-kissed cheekbone.

Einari produced a razor from the pocket of his suit jacket. No robes today. The warehouse's rubble must have ruined his traditional attire. What he wore now was far more modern. His suit was crisp and pristine, dyed a rich ocean blue. He pricked his thumb, and gold beaded to the surface of his skin. The beggar held up a small glass jar, and Einari brushed his thumb against the lip. His blood dripped down the jar's glass slope, pooling in a thin layer at the bottom.

"Thank you, thank you, thank you," gasped the beggar, clutching the jar close to their chest. They bowed as low as they could, their nose kissing the damp dirt below them. *"Kind Einari, merciful Einari..."*

Einari stood tall, reveling in the beggar's praise. A smile graced his lips as he soaked up every drop of the beggar's devotion. If this were a mortal man, Eris would have scoffed, but he did not once think Einari haughty—he *was* a god, after all.

When the beggar sat up, Einari made to leave. He shifted his weight, and his gaze turned upward. As Eris peeled himself from the bridge's ledge, Einari's piercing seafoam green eyes found him. Unsure of what else to do, Eris ran.

3

Eris and Miri were drowning.

Miri had created a spreadsheet, within which hundreds of rows boasted links to blog posts, articles, and newspaper publications, all published within the past two days.

Eris had stumbled upon a few more posts while scrolling through his social media feeds instead of paying attention in class. Sniped photos of Einari. People fawning, people fighting. Devotion and apathy. He scrolled through the document, all the way down to row 486, and pasted them in. *486. 487. 488. 489.*

He sat beside Miri in Wayfarer High School's dilapidated library, shifting his weight upon the creaky wooden chair. Its ugly, faded brown padding was lumpy and uncomfortable. With a fed-up groan, he stood and swapped out his chair with one from an adjacent table. Miri watched him with an amused smile.

These days, Eris spent most lunch periods in the library. His lunch didn't line up with Miri's. He had lunch *A*, and Miri had lunch

C. But this was Miri's free period, which she spent amid Wayfarer High's vast expanse of bookshelves and mandated silence.

His teammates, no doubt, were gabbing about him behind his back. *Eris is turning into a nerd,* they might have said. Or, worse, *I think Eris has a crush on Miri.*

Yuck.

"I think we have enough data," Eris said. "There's no way we can keep up with all this. And look at our graph—it's getting crowded."

"I think we need a thousand data points," argued Miri. At this, Eris choked on his chocolate milk, which he wasn't allowed to have in the library. The librarian was rather strict about enforcing the *no-food-or-drinks* rule. But he and Miri had tucked themselves away in the back corner, which the librarian couldn't see from her desk. "Think about it. Midir's population is *billions.* And even if we only survey Anesh, that's still, what, a couple million? Four hundred is a puny slice of that. One thousand isn't much bigger in comparison, but we'll have a wider breadth of data."

"That's so much," Eris groaned.

"We have time. This is our final project. We need to make sure it's good."

"I guess."

"It'll fill up pretty quick. We're already almost halfway."

Miri was right. Halfway wasn't a bad place to be.

When Eris returned home from school, Mom and Dad loaded him and Aria into their car and drove them across town.

Temples of the Sky traditionally were tall structures, reaching high enough to pierce the clouds. Not this one. This temple was puny, blending in with the grayscale corporate buildings it was smushed between. The smallness was one of the few pleasures Eris took in attending. The Big Four's jester did not deserve a temple any grander than this.

Eris sat slumped in the pews toward the front of the temple, his dad's shoulder brushing his. He couldn't stop his eyes from wandering. What else was there to do, after all, when phones were strictly prohibited during service? How was he supposed to keep himself entertained while the priest tried to slop drivel into his ears?

The temple consisted of one single room. Splotches of midtone beige sat atop otherwise pale walls, the mismatched paint thanks to the renovations from a few years back. They'd knocked out as many interior walls as they could, destroying private prayer rooms to make the nave as large as possible. Nobody could match the original paint color, and it seemed nobody wanted to repaint the whole temple, either. Or, more likely, the temple couldn't afford a new paint job after the construction bills came through.

As far as Eris was aware, the government offered little funding for Temples of the Sky, and priests were not allowed to take money from members, either. Mandated limits on Aeris's worship.

As it should be.

At the front of the temple stood a dais. The lectern was empty, so far as Eris could tell. Most temples kept their god's Book upon the lectern at all hours. Aeris did not have a Book.

A priest, dressed in sky blue vestments, climbed upon the dais. He cradled the Book of the Tide with great care, and when he deposited it onto the lectern, he took a moment to flip through its pages in search of whatever passages he planned to preach about.

There was a particular creativity necessary to be a priest of the sky. The Book of the Tide preached to Aeris's uselessness, and somehow, these priests found positivity to glean from it.

"Good evening," the priest greeted. The quiet murmurs of small talk went quiet. He turned his gaze up, toward the skylight windows above. "What a pleasant day to be worshipping the sky! Not a cloud in sight, allowing us to look upon the stars—and what a blessing it is that they may grace our eyes."

"A blessing, indeed," the temple's patrons echoed. Eris remained quiet, despite his dad nudging him with his elbow. There were few enough people present that Eris could make out individual voices, if he so chose. Another perk to worshipping the sky, Eris supposed. A worship space guaranteed to be quiet and empty.

"Let us begin with a prayer," the priest directed. Eris's family ducked their heads and clasped their hands. "Aeris, we thank you for the air we breathe, the rain that nourishes our crops, the sun that warms our skin, for we could not survive in your absence..."

Usually, Eris would abstain from following along with prayer, hoping his intent would be enough to make it clear to the gods he was not participating. Today, though, he ducked his head and clasped his hands, mirroring everyone else. As the priest led a prayer to the god of the sky, Eris prayed to Einari.

"My king," Eris muttered under his breath. "You grace Midir with your presence, and yet these idiots still worship your jester. Pardon my tongue, but I think you know it's true. These people know your power and reject it. But I know your power and embrace it. I've seen you heal people. I've seen you change lives. Has Aeris changed lives? No."

Eris paused. He tapped his foot. He needed to get the timing of his prayer right. Finish too soon, and he'd have to listen to the rest of the priest's prayer. Finish too late, and his delay would not go unnoticed.

"Aeris breathes precious air and offers nothing in return. Like— oh, what was it? Book of the Tide, page thirty-seven, line... thirteen, I think. Uh, shoot. I don't have the quote memorized. But, the basic gist of it went something like this. Aeris requested a drop of silver to build a small reflecting pool, from which to watch the mortals below. You held out a hand and expected something in return. But Aeris had nothing to provide, and you laughed, and laughed, and laughed.

"Is it a sin to pray to one god while in the home of another? If it is, I hope you'll sympathize when I say I do not care. Someday, I will have the freedom to pray to you from your own temple."

Eris's voice joined dozens of others as he said, "May it be so."

He observed the folks around him. Most sat at the edge of their seats, their eyes alight with devotion, inspiration. Eris did not pay attention to the priest's sermon, but occasionally a few words slipped into his awareness. "The sky is our freedom," the priest proclaimed, gesticulating with the wild fervor of a man who devoted his entire life to the gods. "You must ask yourself in your day-to-day, 'am I allowing myself to be free?' If not, what must you change?"

A lot, Eris thought.

Section 1: Spiritual Presence

Divine presence comes in a lot of different forms. The first form we're going to discuss is spiritual presence. We will define spiritual presence as a metaphysical presence, where the god is not actually there, but people believe in them enough that they are actually kinda there. [User Miri Chase commented: awkward phrasing]

Places where spiritual presence is strongest are in temples. Temples are constructed specifically to evoke spiritual presence. In the Temple of the God King, the high ceilings and murals and stained glass are all meant to bring out a feeling that you're in, or near, the Heavens themselves. Meanwhile, the Temple of the Sky on West Ivory Street is small, but its glass ceiling is designed to bring patrons to a closer relationship with the sky. These aspects are what create a sense of wonder and holiness in people. Architecture, along with strong faith, are the reasons why temples have such a strong spiritual presence.

So, how does spiritual presence affect human behavior?

Eris wanted to smack his head against his blue-gray bedroom wall. How *did* spiritual presence affect human behavior? He stared at his screen, his eyes unfocused. All he'd observed in the Temple of the Sky was people doing their usual prayer. Nothing any less ordinary than walking down the street or doing their taxes. Prayer was as much a routine as it was genuine faith. That was why Mom and Dad always took him to the midweek evening sermons. Routine.

In spiritual spaces, people are a little bit gentler. Like they're walking in the rain, careful not to fall into a puddle, or something. Faith is slippery like that. People are calm when they step into a temple. Maybe they just want to impress the gods, who might be watching them from the Heavens.

He left it at that. Miri could swing by later and add in a few facts and sources. She was phenomenal at digging precise data out of their ever-growing spreadsheet. They were close to one thousand sources, now, and their graph was a crowded disaster.

There were two variables on the graph. The Y axis measured faith. The X axis measured excitement. The lower the level of faith, the less excited people were about Einari's presence. The higher the faith, the higher the excitement. There were a few outliers, of course—a couple of religious folk who dreaded the coming of Einari, believing it an omen, and a few atheists who were rather intrigued by the concept of a real-life god.

Eris did not log his own belief, unsure if he would unintentionally skew the data, but he knew where he'd land on the graph. Average level of faith, high excitement.

He closed the draft and the spreadsheet, then texted Miri to give it a look whenever she got the chance.

Miri replied an hour later. *Will do. Check out this video.*

The footage was shaky and in poor resolution, shot on somebody's phone camera. A massive crowd had gathered by the town square fountain. The cameraperson stood toward the back, camera raised aloft to film over the heads of the folks in front of them.

Einari stood atop the fountain's ledge, its ornate marble carvings and bubbling water made him look bigger, stronger, grander.

"As a reward for your devotion, I have graced Midir with my presence," Einari announced. The audio quality wasn't fantastic. What was it like, Eris wondered, to have been there? Did his voice fill every atom of stagnant air? Was it rich? Grand? It must have been. "I have heard your pleas. I have healed your sick, your injured. Continue devoting yourself to me, and you shall be rewarded! Bountiful clean water to drink! Calm oceans! Give yourselves to me, and I will give myself to you."

Someone in the front row grabbed Einari's leg, snaking her hands around his shin, his calf. Instead of shooing her away, Einari turned his gaze to her, smiled, then offered a hand. She took it without any hesitation, and he helped her up to the ledge.

"What is your name?" Einari asked.

"Aliz," she replied.

"What is your faith?"

"I pray at your temple twice a week."

"And what do you desire?"

"I cannot afford an education. I want to be a historian, but school costs too much."

Einari nodded. He reached into the inner pocket of his coat and produced a tiny jar, so small he could hold it between his thumb and forefinger. He pricked his finger, and golden blood dripped inside.

"Keep this close," he instructed as he pressed it into her palm. "You may find someone willing enough to finance your schooling in exchange."

"Thank you," she said. She offered Einari a bow, then hopped off the fountain's ledge, fingers clasped tight around the little jar, which she held close to her chest. A few people grasped at her, wanting to lay hands upon the divine blood she now possessed. The woman turned away, clutching her prize ever tighter, and scurried away from the crowd.

"Who is next?" Einari called.

"I have endometriosis," said one voice among the crowd. "Doctors won't listen to me, and I'm in a lot of pain."

"Chronic conditions are tricky," Einari mused. "Curing you would take a lot. More than I can offer. But I can lessen your pain."

More people. *I have a headache,* and *My sister can't make rent,* and *Next year, I'm traveling across Midir. I need to save enough money.*

The whole crowd clamored for a share of Einari's blood, but Einari only had so much he could give. People pushed and shoved with unquenchable *need,* desperate to lay their hands upon divine flesh. Even from a distance, Einari's darting eyes were unmistakable. The God

King took a shuffle-step backwards, leaving him teetering on the fountain's ledge. The prospect of getting his feet wet did not deter him. When the crowd surged forward, he stepped into the shallow pool to escape the wall of grabbing hands. Water drenched the hem of his pants.

Someone threw a rock, which whizzed past Einari's head. A near-miss. Einari flinched. A few in the crowd gasped. Others yelled, and whether the yells were of outrage or excitement, Eris could not tell. People pushed and fought one another. One man punched another, and when the victim clutched his face in agony, the aggressor shoved his way forward.

Amid the chaos, Einari slipped away. Moments later, someone bumped into the cameraperson, and they dropped their phone. The video went black.

Eris sat back in his seat. *Wow,* he texted Miri. *This is horrible. Have you read the article?*

Not yet.

Three people were hospitalized. For a few minutes, Eris watched the little dots that indicated she was typing. She would type, then stop, then type again. *Trampled by the crowd. Einari offered no blood to help them.* Another pause. Another too-long stretch of typing. *At what point does faith override logic? At what point does desire turn into desperation?*

Eris did not reply. He wasn't sure what to say. Maybe if he waited long enough, Miri would say something else. Or they'd both go their separate ways.

His phone buzzed again.

At what point does devotion turn into devastation?

4

57th Dew, Prosperity 2192

On the day first drafts were due, a man assaulted Einari.

Eris's parents had a knack for leaving the TV on even when they weren't in the room—a habit Eris usually detested. Today, though, as he spread apple butter on a slice of toast, he peered into the living room to watch the newscaster report the event. Einari had been walking an empty street when a man approached him, brandishing a knife. A nearby bank's security cameras had caught the altercation in grainy black-and-white.

The man wasn't built for a fight. He was scrawny and his hand shook so badly that even the low-quality camera picked up on it—he was not nearly strong enough to confront a god. Einari slipped away, unscathed.

When Eris placed his and Miri's draft in the homework basket on Mr. Darren's desk, rendered inaccurate in a matter of days, he exchanged a knowing glance with Miri. And at lunchtime, Eris rushed to the library without bothering to wait in the cafeteria line. Miri offered him a bag of fruit snacks from her lunchbox.

"We can't keep up with all of this," Eris said, peeling open the colorful plastic packaging. "Our graph is useless to us now. A thousand data points about *excitement*—we need new data, tracking the elapsed time since Einari's arrival, and the number of times people have acted out, or whatever."

"We're only on our first draft. We've got until the first of Sun to solidify things. That's, like, four weeks away. Four and a half, I guess. We have time. If we have to completely rewrite, we will."

"Let's get to work, then."

Miri started a new document and copied their first draft into it. "Version history," she explained. "If we cut something that we realize we need, we can go back and grab it from the other draft."

"You think of everything, don't you?"

Miri laughed and rolled her eyes. "Not nearly. Remind me to tell you about the science fair Papa and Dad took me to a few years ago."

"Noted."

"Anyway," Miri said. "I think we can keep a lot of this, we'll just need to condense it. We'll have one section about the rise of excitement and devotion as word spread, and then we'll dedicate the rest to... everything else."

"Okay. Yeah. That's doable."

Miri and Eris chopped apart and reordered their draft. They deleted the entire section about spiritual presence, deeming it unnecessary in the paper's grander context. From there, they reorganized everything else. They deleted data. They reworded paragraphs.

Somewhere along the way, Eris looked at his watch and gasped. "Shoot. I'm way late for class. I was supposed to be there half an hour ago."

"Oh," Miri said, eyeing him. "We should've set an alarm."

What was the merit in showing up now? The best that would happen was an embarrassing lecture from his teacher and a walk of shame to his desk. He could endure humiliation, or...

"I'll stay for the rest of the period," Eris said.

"Are you sure?"

"Positive."

They worked in moderate silence, save for the occasional, *"Hey, look at this."* When the bell rang, Eris tucked his laptop into his bag and headed to his next class.

Algebra didn't matter, anyway. The only reason he planned to go to college was for lacrosse. He'd survive if he missed one boring lecture about solving equations.

After school, Mom and Dad perched at the kitchen table, poised to intercept him the moment he stepped through the door. *Drat.* He let his backpack slide off his shoulder, and onto the floor beside the stairwell.

"We got a call from the school," Dad said. "You skipped mathematics today."

Eris winced. "I didn't mean to. I was working on my science project with Miri. I lost track of time."

"Eris, your grades are slipping. Is everything okay?"

"Everything's fine."

Mom, ever the practical one, leaned one elbow on the kitchen table and said, "We're worried you won't get accepted into any colleges if you don't get your grades up."

All I need to do is ace tryouts, and I'll be in. Eris didn't dare speak those words aloud. His parents would be inclined to disagree.

"We want to see you succeed. No more skipping class, you hear? Your dad and I agreed to let you off on a warning, this time, but if it happens again, you're grounded."

"Okay," Eris grumbled. He averted his gaze, opting instead to stare at the layer of dust gathering on the baseboards. Mom gave him a firm pat on the shoulder, and that was that.

Eris walked to the town square that evening. He had not planned to meet up with Miri, but he found her there, knelt upon the decorative cobblestone pavement, eyeing an off-colored splotch. Evidence of spilled blood. Mortal blood.

"Hey, Miri," Eris greeted. "I guess we had the same thought, huh?"

Miri looked up, startled. "Oh. Yeah. Guess so."

"I have to admit, the recent developments with Einari have been... a bit depressing. Don't you think? I don't want this to become a pattern."

"It will."

Eris tapped his toe against the ground, adjusting where his shoe sat on his foot. "I think we need to find him. For real, this time. We could talk to him."

Miri stood. "Interview him?"

"No. Not even that. He's a god, we can't treat him like data. Just... I don't know. Reassure him that not all mortals demand things of him, you know? I don't want him leaving Midir with a sour taste on his tongue."

Miri nodded. She retrieved her phone from her pocket and scrolled, pausing only once to nudge her round-framed glasses up her face. Eris opened his mouth, poised to ask her what she was doing.

"Got it," Miri exclaimed before he could get a word out. "Last sighting, posted fifteen minutes ago: near the boardwalk. He may still be there."

Eris nodded. Miri bolted down the street, leaving Eris to scramble after her.

On the horizon, the city skyline gave way to an endless expanse of water. What a blessing it was, to live in a city along the ocean. The glittering waters constituted a breathtaking view, with waves greeting him on his bus ride to school every day—sometimes gentle and sometimes rough, determined by Einari's mood on any given day. The ocean served as a close, easy vacation spot, too, so long as one was willing to put up with the swarms of half-naked, sunburnt people sprawled across the sandy beaches.

A nigh-endless boardwalk stretched across the beach, spanning what Eris could only presume was the length of Anesh's borders, if not further. Eris had never bothered to explore it, despite having lived in the city for many years. Someday, in an act of devotion to Einari, he would. Once his parents stopped forcing him to worship Aeris.

Finding Einari was not a difficult endeavor. Miri spotted people standing on the pothole-ridden street parallel to the boardwalk. This was hardly a prime hang-out spot—that could only mean Einari was there.

Miri kept along the sidewalks, walking tight against the adjacent buildings, her shoulder brushing against brickwork and vinyl siding. She motioned for Eris to do the same. *Keep away,* her gesture stated. *I don't want us getting trampled.*

They inched closer to the bustling crowd. These folks weren't poor, weren't ill, weren't wounded. All Eris needed was one glance to clock these people as being middle- and upper-class, wearing colorful swimsuits, jogging gear, and fancy work clothes. A sinking feeling settled within Eris. While there were needy folks in the world who would tangibly benefit from a share of Einari's blood, these people wanted to make a profit. That's how things always seemed to go, these days. No venture was worthwhile unless it made money.

Though Einari held a poised, dignified posture, there was a firm tension in his shoulders. His brow was creased, the bridge of his nose crinkled. Eris, instead of approaching the overwhelmed god, dipped into the nearest alleyway. Miri glanced over her shoulder at Einari, then back to Eris, with a frown. Hesitant to follow, she lingered on the sidewalk.

Eris searched up and down the length of the alley. No other people were present to interfere—just a bunch of rancid trash cans and a raccoon that did not appear spooked by Eris's presence. A small, quiet street intersected the alley. *Perfect.*

"This'll work," Eris announced.

"What'll work?"

"Escape route."

Miri nodded. She turned back toward the crowd, toward Einari, who took two steps back for every one step the crowd took forward. She waved with large, broad, overhead motions.

"Einari!" Miri shouted. "Your Grace, over here!" Miri's voice melded with the crowd, lost among the clamor. Her voice was light and airy—Eris wasn't sure he'd ever heard her truly yell. Even now, her shout was small. Still, she forced herself to call louder, firmer. "Your Grace!"

Einari's gaze flitted over to the alley. Eris gestured for him to come, and Einari narrowed his eyes in mistrust. This plan was a poor one. Why would Einari trust two mortals in a dark alley? What good could ever come of something like that?

But Einari seemed to be weighing his options, so far as Eris could tell, his attention shifting back to the crowd, then to the alley once more. Eris could only imagine what was going on in his mind: *What's worse: being trampled by a crowd, or being knifed in seclusion?*

Einari pricked his thumb with the razorblade he kept in his coat pocket. *Why?* It seemed the opposite of what Einari wished to accomplish. The crowd grabbed for his bloodied hand. As people surged, so did the tide. With a flick of his wrist, Einari raised a wave taller than any Eris had seen before. The wave's long shadow stretched across the beach. The boardwalk. The street. With the crowd skittering away, frightened by the waterlogged doom the wave imposed, Einari slipped into the alley.

The wave crashed upon the street, drenching the few people who had remained. Water lapped at Eris's feet, seeping through the mesh of his shoes. "Come this way," Eris urged as he hurried down the alley, fighting to ignore the visceral *squelch* of waterlogged socks. He swung around the corner, onto the quiet side street. "We can get you somewhere safe."

Einari did not move with the same urgency Eris did. He walked, his posture firm, a fist clenched, poised to defend himself.

"There's a pedestrian underpass at the end of this road," Eris explained. "It'll lead you to the other side of town."

"What do you expect to gain in return?" Einari's voice took on a low, cautious timbre. He kept a few paces behind Eris and Miri, far enough back that Eris needed to turn his head to ensure Einari was still following.

"Nothing," Eris said.

"Nothing?" Einari repeated, skepticism thick in his deep voice.

"Nothing, Your Grace."

"All mortals want something."

"I want for you, when you go back to the Heavens, to remember those who helped you, not just those who hurt you."

Einari did not reply with any immediacy, so Eris forged the path onward. He led the god of the sea down the road, his trembling hands tucked into his pockets. The man walking behind him was a god. A *god!* How was he supposed to behave? How could he possibly make up for the attacks? The lack of respect?

"...We shall see," Einari eventually grumbled. His voice was thick and low with mistrust.

An archway loomed overhead, cutting across the empty back street. On the bridge above, cars sat bumper to bumper. Honks punctuated the thrum of engines. Eris gestured to the pedestrian underpass.

"Through here, you'll get to the Kinkade district. I can't guarantee more people won't try to swarm you, though. You should find some new clothes, something that will help you blend in—"

"Tell me," Einari asked. "What are your names?"

"I'm..." Eris hesitated. He couldn't stomach the idea of telling Einari his given name. But to lie to a god? Would that be worse? "I'm John."

"Miri."

"Well, John and Miri, if you are right about mortals showing kindness, there should be no reason to hide." Einari paused. "And if you are wrong..."

Eris shivered under Einari's steely, authoritative gaze. He had half a heart to bow before the God King now, to beg forgiveness. He had not meant to offend. But Einari turned his attention to the underpass before Eris could follow through.

Einari took a single step forward. The archway's curved shadow cast itself across his face like shroud. "...Then, such will be immediately apparent."

The God King swept away, ocean-blue coattails billowing behind him.

5

Sitting through school was excruciating when Eris's phone vibrated hourly. He'd signed up for notifications from four different news sources, which all posted articles about Einari—and only Einari, as any other newsworthy event paled in comparison to the presence of a god— at regular intervals throughout the day.

Phones weren't allowed in school, and Eris knew he risked detention, but he couldn't help but sneak a peek when he could. *Victim of Crowd Trampling Offers Warning,* or *Suspect of Einari's Attempted Stabbing Apprehended,* or *Words of Warning from Einari: "Mind Yourselves, Sinners."*

The worst, though, came at the end of the day, while Eris waited for his bus to open its doors. Why the buses congregated in the lot with their doors shut, not letting students board, was beyond Eris. At the very least, though, the bus drivers' obnoxious little rule left Eris time to socialize. Instead of standing with his teammates, like he usually did, he sat on a concrete bench with Miri. He found he'd rather hang out with her. His teammates were teammates in the same way his classmates were classmates. Acquaintances.

He was in the middle of telling Miri about a video game he thought she might enjoy. A conversation so mundane was a welcome reprieve, all things considered. When he felt his phone buzz, he snuck a glance. "The final boss is the best," he was saying. "I won't spoil it, but his character design is really cool…"

He trailed off.

"Everything okay?" Miri asked with a small frown.

"Data Measured by Midir International Science Association Indicates Global Rise in Sea Level," Eris read. *"Climate Fluctuation, or Angry God?"*

"I saw the data earlier, straight off MISA's website," Miri said. "It's not as bad as it sounds. It's more likely to be a natural fluctuation."

"I hope so," Eris muttered. He watched as all the buses opened their doors in sync. Most students were eager to board the moment they were allowed, but Eris lingered on the bench with Miri a while longer. "Should we include this in our report?"

"No. Our report's about human behavior, not ecology."

"Right." Eris stood and slung his backpack over one shoulder. "I'll see you tomorrow. I'll try to get some more work done on the paper tonight, assuming Mom and Dad don't force me to do chores or look after my sister."

"Hey." Miri caught his arm before he could step away. Her fingers were warm and soft against the tender skin of his wrist. "Let's ditch school tomorrow."

"You... want to ditch?" Eris repeated, astonished.

"I can't shake the feeling we've made the situation worse. We have to try, just one more time, to get through to him." She chewed on her lower lip. "I... Eris, I can't sleep at night. I keep worrying. What if he goes back to the Heavens angry? What will he do to us? What if he punishes us, but that punishment is entirely preventable? What if we're not trying hard enough?"

Eris nodded. "Let's ditch, then. Let me know where you want to meet, and I'll be there."

"See you tomorrow."

Eris left Miri at the bench and boarded his bus. He stared out the small, stained window, wondering which bus she usually took. He never found out. When the bus doors slid closed, Miri was still sitting there, alone, on that bench.

He had a sinking feeling that she hadn't arranged for her dads to pick her up.

Eris snuck out of the house while his parents were busy freshening up for work. Getting away with the deed was easy. All he had to do was call up the stairs, "Mom, Dad, I'm meeting Miri before school. Her dad is picking me up. See you later!"

And then, he was free.

Miri had not texted him a meetup spot yet. She was probably too busy trying to convince her own parents to take their eyes off her long enough to sneak away. Regardless, Eris needed to get away from the neighborhood, and fast, lest his parents find out he'd lied, so he speed-walked through the city streets. He picked up a few pieces of trash he found on the ground and dumped them into the closest receptacle. His hands felt grimy after touching weather-worn plastic bags and cardboard, but he ignored the sensation of dirt on his fingers as best he could.

He wound up at the town square. This morning, the space was quiet, not another soul out enjoying the warm dew season air. There was no time nor reason to linger and socialize. Right now, everyone was rushing to school or work.

Eris didn't mind sitting alone. He found a table near the fountain and watched the water spray from its many decorative spouts, pooling into the basin below, whose bottom layer glinted with the metallic shine of pennies.

On his phone, he opened a game he only played on long car drives or in waiting rooms. Sorting blocks of color into their respective bins wasn't the most exciting thing he could do, but it helped fill the time well enough. Better than staring at the sky and twiddling his thumbs.

A little past the top of the hour, Miri texted. *Meet me at Southside. Right by Benny's Books.*

Eris hopped from his seat and ran. He wasn't sure he could stomach walking. Too much time wasted. A jog would help get some of his nervous energy out, anyhow. Gods knew he had a lot of it these days.

Benny's Books was half-cafe, half-bookstore. Eris didn't like reading, so he'd never considered visiting this place before, but it seemed quaint. Judging by how Miri stood with a book peeking out of her tote bag and a bubbly drink in her hand, she must enjoy the place.

He wiped a bead of sweat from his brow and attempted to calm his breathing as he approached. He offered Miri a wave. "Hey."

"Hey," she replied. "I heard word that Einari was passing through here a little while ago. It might be too late, now, but it's a good place to start, if nothing else. We've got all day to track him down."

"And what are we going to do when we find him?"

Miri smiled. She reached into her tote and pulled out a small plastic bag, no wider than Eris's palm. Inside it was a handful of shells, which were painted with vibrant, whimsical patterns, as well as a few sea salt caramels.

"We're going to make sure he enjoys his trip."

"No offense, but I don't think seashells and candy will appease a god."

"I know, but I can't afford much else. I was hoping he'd be the kind of god who appreciates any gift, so long as there's faith put into it."

"Maybe," Eris mused. "Or he's too overwhelmed to care. I guess we may as well try."

"Once more," Miri said, closing her eyes for a moment and tilting her head back, toward the sky, either to ready herself or to pay a brief respect to the Heavens above. "Let's track down a god."

Southside was a bust—the rumor Miri was banking on was too old, now, outdated in a matter of minutes. Einari was long gone. They combed the streets, peering through every alleyway, every window. Miri kept her phone in her hand, glancing at it every now and then. Someone posted a photo of Einari on Freymore Street, and forty minutes later, on the intersection between 18th and Ironwood.

Eris's calves were sore by lunchtime. He and Miri stopped at some cheap fast-food joint to buy burgers to go. They ate while they crossed the bridge out of Southside and back into the Central Quarter. The burger tasted like ash and salt.

"What if we don't find him?" Eris asked. "It's silly of us to think we'll have the same luck again. We're chasing one single guy."

"I refuse to let today go to waste. I've never skipped school before, and I don't ever want to do it again. We *need* to find him."

They fell into focused silence. Every once in a while, Miri would call out a post she found, something like, *I can't believe Einari is in my neighborhood!* Or *I just saw Einari near that public shrine by the government center.* Eris and Miri would then change course and head to the next street or landmark.

"We have to be getting closer," Miri said, her voice light with hope, despite the heaviness of exhaustion weighing down on both of them. She was right. In the morning, they'd had to cut across town, backtrack, or cross district lines in order to keep pace. Now, though, they were following a small, interlocking series of roads.

Eris caught a fleeting glimpse of Einari turning down a side street. He appeared to be in a rush, casting a glance over his shoulder as he swung around the corner. His usually pristine black hair was a tangled, windswept mess.

Another man turned the corner, in pursuit of the God King. He was gone before Eris could get a good look at his face. All Eris saw was a mop of curly brown hair, the man's black long-sleeved shirt, rolled up to the elbow in the late dew season warmth, and his ripped jeans.

And the pistol in the man's hand.

Fear shot through Eris. *I should get out of here before he shoots me, too,* he thought. Then, *No. We need to help Einari.*

Eris took off into a run, Miri behind him. He whirled around the corner, following them onto the side street. They weaved and ducked through alleys, between yards, across roads. Gunshots ripped through the air. A bullet smashed through an office building's window; another ricocheted against a steel storm drain. Eris, on instinct, shielded his head with his hands. Not that such a gesture would protect him much.

Another gunshot. This one hit its mark.

Einari collapsed face-first on the pavement with a choked shout. Divine golden blood pooled on the asphalt from a wound in his back. The man rushed to Einari, pulling plastic bottles from his satchel. He siphoned as much blood into the bottles as he could manage. Einari writhed and gasped in agony. His pained eyes met Eris's, gaze hardening in recognition.

Eris couldn't move. Miri, beside him, held her hands to her mouth, her sage green eyes shimmering with terror. Should he call the police? The hospital? But what could any mortal do to save a dying god? A blood transfusion only worked if there was blood on hand to offer, and no God's Blood existed on Midir aside from Einari's.

Einari's body fell still. The shine left his eyes. Eris grabbed Miri's hand, hoping it would quell the way he trembled. All the gesture served to do, however, was compound her nerves with his.

"We should go," Miri whispered. She tugged at Eris's hand, but he couldn't bring himself to move.

When Einari's murderer turned around, Eris caught sight of his face. Freckles dotted his square jaw, his upper lip punctuated by a well-maintained mustache.

Only then did Eris allow himself to run.

Eris trudged into his house, numb. In the living room, he found Aria playing with some toy trains. He knelt beside his sister and gave her a tight hug. Embracing her was the only thing he could think to do.

Aria squealed, then giggled and squeezed him back. He didn't acknowledge his little sister often. Hugging her was nice, though. Warm. Far warmer than anything Dad would give him, if the manner in which he peered over his newspaper from his perch on the couch was any indication.

"Play with me?" Aria asked.

"Sure." Eris sat up straight and place a trembling hand on one of Aria's little plastic trains. Playing little kid games was embarrassing, but it would be a good way to fend off the flashes of Einari's corpse, the man stealing golden blood from the God King himself...

Dad cleared his throat. Eris looked up from the toys on the floor.

"The school informed me that you didn't show up to any of your classes today," he said. Eris slumped. "This recent behavior is unacceptable. You're grounded."

"Dad, I—"

"Don't talk back. No video games, no going out with friends. Either Mom or I will drive you to school every day."

I watched a god die today. Grounding felt so inconsequential. He rolled the little plastic train across the rug.

"No, not like that!" Aria exclaimed with a pout. "It can't go that way. There's no tracks there."

Eris eyed the floor. Five little trains sat in sporadic places upon the cream-colored rug. "Where are the tracks, then?"

Aria pointed at an arbitrary spot. "There!"

Eris placed the train on its imaginary track. He paused, narrowed his eyes, then looked at Aria with as serious a face as he could muster. "But what about the monster on the track?"

"Monster?"

"Look!" Eris planted his elbow upon the rug, angling his hand so his fingers made the shape of a horned creature. Moving his fingers, he opened and closed the creature's mouth. *"Rawr! I'm hungry!"*

"Nooo!" Aria exclaimed. "It's okay! There's a god here. He'll save the day."

Dead, unblinking eyes. Golden blood. Twitching fingers, the last light of life fading from a crumpled corpse. Eris forced a smile. "A god? Which one?"

"Um..." She hesitated. "George."

"George? What's George the god of?"

"Trains."

Eris snickered. "Sure, sure."

GOD KING FOUND DEAD ON ANESH STREET

Eris lay on his bed, his lights long since turned off. He'd been watching brainless videos, grateful his parents had the mind not to confiscate his phone. The notification startled him, as he wasn't expecting any news platform to publish an article so late into the night.

The article detailed what Eris had witnessed, though sparing the gruesome details. *Einari's body was discovered in an alley near the boardwalk at 6:45 p.m., bearing a gunshot wound to the back. Autopsy reports confirm the bullet pierced his lungs. The killer is still at large, and investigations are ongoing.*

He shivered. He should email the investigator, provide a description of the killer's face. Or he could ignore the situation and hope to awaken in a world where everything was fine.

Unsure of what else to do, Eris texted Miri. *I'm grounded for skipping school.*

Miri replied almost immediately. *Sorry. It would've been better if we hadn't ditched.* And then, a minute later, *I can't stop thinking about it.*

Neither could Eris. He did not reply. He couldn't.

Instead, he rose from his bed and found his place at his desk. He booted up his computer and opened a blank document. At the top of the document, he wrote: *Tree Biodiversity's Impact on Local Squirrel Populations.*

6

When Eris awoke, his second-story bedroom was a touch warmer than usual. The cooling unit was not humming its usual hum.

He kicked his blankets off, displeased to wake up sweaty. No matter—he could remedy the situation with a long morning jog and a cold shower.

If Mom and Dad allowed him out of the house.

Eris stepped into the hallway and flipped the light switch. The lights did not turn on. He frowned. *Oddly clear day for a power outage.* He made for the stairs, his stomach growling. With the power out, he wouldn't have much luck with breakfast. The toaster wouldn't work, so he couldn't have a bagel, and the milk in the fridge may have gone bad—

Halfway down the stairs, he froze.

Water lapped at the fourth step from the bottom, briny and brown. The walls were pinkish with mildew.

"Uh, Mom?" Eris called. "Dad?"

Silence.

Eris ran back upstairs. He rushed to his bedroom and peered out his window. The streets were a swimming pool of brackish water. Fish flitted within.

Yesterday, Anesh sat at sea level. Today, it was below.

Eris ran for Mom and Dad's bedroom door at the end of the hall. He pounded his fist against it. From inside, he heard a shuffling sound, and moments later the door creaked open.

"Eris, it's the weekend," Mom complained. She blinked slowly and rubbed the sleep from her eyes. "What is it?"

"The house is flooded," Eris gasped. "The whole first floor. Power's out, too."

This seemed to snap Mom awake. She tried the light switch by the door, flipping it on, off, on, off. Nothing. She rushed to the window and threw open the curtains. Sunlight flooded the bedroom.

"Oh, dear," she gasped.

"What do we do?" Eris asked. "We can't drive anywhere. The car..." He couldn't bring himself to finish his sentence. Outside, water overtook rubber tires and lapped at the car's exterior.

"We'll just sit tight," Dad said as he climbed out of bed. "It'll go away in a few days."

Eris wasn't sure he could sit tight, but grounded and trapped as he was, sitting tight was all he could do. He trudged back to his bedroom and shut off his laptop, hoping to preserve power. He wouldn't be able to recharge until after the water receded. *If* the water receded.

Are you okay? He texted Miri.

Okay as can be, all things considered, she replied. *I told Papa and Dad what we saw. I think they're a little freaked out. Can't tell if it's because of the flooding or because I was so close to danger.*

A pause.

Are you okay?

Hanging in there, Eris replied. *Power's out. I'm gonna shut off my phone. I'll text you tonight.*

He did not wait for Miri to reply. He held the power button until the screen went black, then set it on his desk, resolving to scavenge for breakfast.

Wading through waist-deep water in his own home was a miserable venture. The water was frigid and grimy, having picked up all the dirt and oil on the streets. He sloshed through the hallway, arms bent at the elbows to keep his hands dry.

The cupboards beneath the countertop were all waterlogged. The freezer was below the waterline, and Eris was hesitant to open it, not eager to let the cold out and the water in. That was, of course, assuming the freezer's contents weren't already drenched. He waded his way to the pantry. One box of oat cereal sat on the top shelf, out of the water's reach. Eris snagged it and a bag of chocolate chips, below the water but sealed in airtight plastic packaging, then headed back upstairs.

As the day wore on, the water level rose. For a while, the water was higher outside than it was inside, but by the afternoon one of the downstairs windows cracked, then shattered. Water poured in, carrying shards of glass with it.

At dinnertime, Mom braved the waters and retrieved a bag of frozen dumplings, which they couldn't eat until past midnight, when they had thawed enough to bite into.

His curiosity got the better of him later that evening. He turned his phone on. Its battery was at sixty percent. *Must not have charged long last night,* Eris realized with a grimace.

No texts from Miri. He sent her a message. *You okay?*

He did not get an immediate reply. He tried not to worry, especially as he scrolled through the latest news articles.

Coastal Cities Anesh, Medán, Yenia, Among Others Devastated by Rising Sea Levels

Thousands Dead from Sea God's Rage

Get to Higher Ground: Evacuation Orders Released for Residents of Medán, Anesh

How was evacuation even possible? Unless some charitable neighbor owned a boat, they weren't going anywhere. He was stuck in this house, waiting to die.

The notion was not a reassuring one.

Sleep came fitful at best. He woke every hour, paranoid that at any moment water might reach the second story. His phone vibrated sometime in the dead of night. Unable to sleep, he rolled over and checked the notification.

Not really, Miri had replied. *Papa just suggested we climb to the roof. I'm scared.*

Me too, Eris replied.

He shut off his phone and squeezed his eyes shut, hoping for sleep that never came. He found himself listening to the sounds of seawater lapping at the house, inside and outside.

At some point, Mom and Dad burst into his room, Aria cradled in Dad's arms. Their silhouettes were illuminated only by the dim moonlight streaming through the windows.

"Eris, come," Mom gasped. "We need to get to the roof. We'll be safe there."

Will we? Eris thought, but he hopped to his feet and hurried down the hall into the spare room at the end. Dad hiked up the dormer window and gestured for everyone to climb out.

Eris went first. He squeezed through the window and out onto the roof, his balance wobbly upon the steep, slick tiles. The air outside tasted salty, humid. He extended his hands, and Dad passed Aria through the window. Eris held her tight as he climbed the roof. He settled at its apex, where the ridge's sharp edge prodded him.

Aria was crying. Not her usual wails, but a small, sniffling kind of cry, which soaked the collar of Eris's shirt. He tried to set her down upon the rooftop, but she refused to let go, so he let her squeeze him until Mom and Dad arrived. When they did, Eris coaxed Aria off him and onto Mom's lap instead. He rested his elbows on his knees and stared out at the wasteland that had once been his neighborhood.

The houses had become a series of islands. Some people occupied their roofs, like the Vandermere family now did. Some roofs were empty, like the one across the street, which was home to a kid two years younger than him. When Eris was in middle school, they used to shoot hoops together on the weekends.

Eris shuddered. Had that family drowned? Or were they lucky enough to be out of town? For their sake, Eris hoped it was the latter, though he could see their car parked in the driveway, submerged below the waves.

There was a high-rise apartment at the end of the road, and through its windows, Eris spotted people scrambling up the countless flights of stairs, bodies crammed against each other. Maybe those people were better off, since they were in a taller building. Or would they die sooner, thanks to the sheer volume of panicked people congesting the narrow stairwell? How many would be trampled? How many would drown?

At least Eris's roof was quiet.

He reached into his pocket, only to find it empty. *Crap.* He eyed the water level, which kissed the lip of the second story windows.

He stood. "I'll be right back."

"Eris, no," Mom snapped. "What are you doing? Stay here."

"I left my phone in my room," he replied. "I need to grab it."

"Leave it. It's not safe."

"If we can call the emergency line, we might be able to get help," Eris snapped. *And I want to make sure Miri's okay.*

He did not wait for permission. He clambered down the side of the roof and back into the house.

The water was above his waist, now, rising higher by the minute. He slogged through the hallway, his breaths coming quick, panicked. *I need to get my phone. I need to get my phone.* He repeated the mantra in his head, drilling it into his core. *Get my phone, get my phone, get my phone.*

The current of water had strewn his belongings around his bedroom, leaving clothes sodden on the floor, a few homework papers floating upon the surface. His laptop sat upon his desk, long ruined. All his hard work, ruined in an instant.

He snatched his phone off the bedside table and hurried out, not eager to linger. Fear of drowning in his own home spurred him onward—the sooner he could get back to the roof, the better. But, as he rushed through the hall, he caught a glimpse of Aria's door and hesitated.

Eris ducked inside. *I'll be quick.* From Aria's bed, pink and yellow sheets unmade, he snatched Mr. Squiggles. Mr. Squiggles, just like the bedroom walls, was covered in marker scribbles in almost every color of the rainbow, save for orange. Aria had never cared much for the color orange.

He folded his hands and prayed. *Have mercy, Einari. Please, have mercy. I am devout to you—and Aria, she's not old enough to know that the god she prays to is a worthless one. Spare us, and she'll learn.*

Eris hurried down the hall in an awkward half-swim, half-walk. Shards of glass drifted through the water. Somewhere, the water pressure had shattered another window. When he reached the guest room's window, the water level was nearing his shoulders, submerging the window's lower pane. He drew a deep breath, then dove underwater and squeezed outside.

Eris resurfaced with a gasp and scrambled up the roof's slope. As he shook his arms dry, all the tension left his parents' shoulders.

He wrung water from Mr. Squiggles and pressed him into Aria's arms. This soothed her crying some. She sniffled and hugged the toy close to her chest. Well-loved, the stuffed bear was, with one of its button eyes falling loose, its seams broken and spilling fluff from within, and its fabric matted and dirty.

Eris pressed his phone's power button. The screen did not light up. With a grimace, he shook the phone, and water dribbled from the charger port. He pressed and held the power button. If he held it long enough, would it turn on?

No luck. Eris tucked it into his pocket. *I'll let it dry for a bit.*

When the sun rose and water nearly encompassed the rooftop, leaving Eris and his family clinging to the chimney, a boat sailed by.

Some neighbor's recreational fishing boat. Its electric motor cut through the haunting silence.

"HELP!" Dad yelled, waving his arms to capture the boater's attention. Mom joined in, screaming and waving, both their voices sharp with desperation. Eris held his breath. Aria squeezed Mr. Squiggles.

The boat came to a stop parallel to the thin strip of remaining roof. While Mom gasped out a long string of thank-yous, Eris regarded the boat, already full of people.

"We don't have space for four more," someone on the boat said. Eris couldn't tell who had spoken.

"We have to try," said another.

"We can't. There's no way."

Eris spotted a face he recognized. A bob of brown hair, round glasses, green eyes. *Miri.*

"We have to help them," Miri exclaimed. "Please. Eris is my friend. I can't leave him."

Mom and Dad exchanged a glance. Mom picked Aria up and pressed her into Eris's arms. Eris frowned at her, nerves bubbling in his chest.

"Eris," Mom said, her voice so gentle, so kind, so calm. "Take your sister and board the boat."

"What about you?" Eris asked, his voice wavering.

"Don't worry about us, hon."

Dad placed a hand on Eris's shoulder. The kind of touch that said, *I'm proud of you.* His smile carried both a loving warmth and a heavy sadness.

"No, no," Eris babbled, "I can't leave you. I can't. We—we'll make room. Please."

The water level was rising, rising. Seawater engulfed the entirety of the roof, and it wouldn't be much longer until they were treading water. Dad nudged him toward the boat. A tall man with broad shoulders and a beard reached down to him from aboard, beckoning him. Eris cast a glance over his shoulder at his parents, then at the man.

What could he do? Board a fishing boat full of strangers? Or die with his parents?

"Go on," Dad urged. "You and Aria... you're everything to us."

"Don't do this." His chest ached. His body was weak, shaky, unreliable. Mom and Dad said nothing, offering the bearded man aboard the boat a solemn nod. The man wrapped a hand around Eris's bicep and pulled him aboard. Eris squeezed amid the others already aboard, and the boat's motor kicked back to life.

As they sailed away, Eris screamed until his voice gave out.

7

Eight people occupied a fishing boat built for six. Eris sat on the floor. Miri had slipped off her seat to join him, and even though she sat in silence, he appreciated her presence.

The sun blared from above, hot and bright, searing the back of Eris's neck. He had sobbed every last tear his body could muster, but still, his lower lip quivered. He had lost sight of his parents quite some time ago. How long had they treaded water before they drowned?

Aria clung to Eris's arm and refused to let go no matter how many times Eris tried to shake her off. "Where's Mommy and Daddy?" she kept asking. Eris grimaced. He wished she would shut up.

"Hey, Papa," Miri called. She caught the bearded man's attention. He seemed to understand, and he scooped Aria into his arms. Eris did not pay attention to what Miri's papa said to her, but he must have come up with some gentle way to tell her she'd never see Mom and Dad again.

"This is our fault," Eris said, his gaze glued to the ocean below him. Dead worms floated in the water, lured out from wet soil, then drowned. "Isn't it?"

"I hope not," Miri replied. She folded her elbows over the boat's guardrail. Her sullen face betrayed her. "We did everything we could."

"Did we, though? We could have saved the world. We're failures, Miri."

Eris reached down and trailed his fingers along the water's surface. Below, Eris glimpsed murky silhouettes of homes and streets, long submerged. Their silhouettes rippled with the tide. They looked so far away.

Aria sat between Miri's dads. They'd employed her to help unspool the fishing line they'd found in storage, which they were attempting to tie to a tree branch. She worked so diligently that she unraveled the entire spool, and Papa, with a laugh, instructed her to re-wrap it before everything got tangled.

"Your dads," Eris muttered, casting a glance at Miri. "They seem in good spirits."

"I'd be surprised if they weren't hurting," Miri replied. "We'd been renting our house for years, and they finally saved enough to buy it off the landlord last year. Only to lose everything they'd worked for."

"I'm sorry."

"But someone's gotta put on a smile for everyone else, y'know? If it weren't for them, I think half of us would've hurled ourselves overboard, wanting to end it."

Eris shuddered at the thought. He might have been one of those people. He missed when being grounded was the worst thing to happen.

He squeezed his eyes shut, and Miri leaned her head against his shoulder.

Miri's dad's name was Rob. Eris learned this when the man—short, stout, bald, and not well-versed in the art of fishing—wrenched a fish from the water with a firm tug. Miri's papa exclaimed, "Nice catch, Rob!" and clapped him on the shoulder with a broad smile, as though this were a causal fishing date and not a means of survival. Eris spotted it, though. The fear. His smile did not reach his eyes, which darted around at the eight occupants, then to the tiny fish, knowing it wouldn't be enough to feed everyone.

The fish flopped around on the sparse amount of deck that wasn't occupied by people's feet. An older lady with a kind, wrinkled face and a shock of white hair, who'd been steering the boat until now, picked the fish up by its tail. "We don't have a way of cooking this, do we?" she asked.

Rob slumped in his seat, his victory short-lived. "Shoot," he said, casting a wayward glance at his husband. "We've got so much hiking gear, and we didn't even think to grab the camp stove from the garage."

"We'll have to eat it raw," Miri's papa concluded, his disgust palpable. He produced a utility knife from his pocket and held out his hand. The woman passed him the fish. Eris looked away, but he couldn't tune out the wet sounds of metal against flesh, fish skin falling upon the deck with a revolting *splat.*

Miri's papa cut the fish into minuscule portions and handed them out to each of the boat's occupants. Eris gagged as he bit into his chunk of the fish. Its meat was slimy and tasted like iron, still bloodied. All he could do was choke it down and hope he didn't get sick.

Eris did not sleep that night. The fishing boat's rigid plastic shell, uncomfortable and rocking with the waves, kept him up. A deep-rooted, profound sadness welled within him. This was the first night he'd ever spent without his parents. Not in a college dorm, but on a boat.

Waiting for sunrise felt like torture. Eris wasn't alone in his restlessness. Miri's papa sat at the bow, staring out at the horizon. Careful not to rock the little boat and wake anyone, Eris tiptoed his way over and sat on the seat beside him.

"Hi," Eris whispered. He perched his feet on the edge of his seat and hugged his knees. The night was so dark Eris could not tell sea from sky. There was only one beacon of light in the distance—some skyscraper that still had electricity.

"The stars are so bright," Mr. Chase muttered. "Now that there's no light on the streets,"

Eris had never seen so many stars before—just the occasional one or two that were bright enough to break through the city lights. Mr. Chase was right. Mom and Dad would have loved to see the vast tapestry of stars glittering against the deep black sky. There were some dim colors, too, purples and blues, which Eris had only ever seen when exaggerated in photographs. Was he staring at an entire galaxy above him? Was that where the Heavens were?

He let himself pray to Aeris. Just this once.

For Mom and Dad's sake, thank you for making the night a touch more bearable. Even though you're doing nothing to help us.

"Miri told me a lot about you," Mr. Chase said. "She's quite fond of you."

"We've gotten close," Eris replied.

"Once this is all over, you better stick close to her. She never had many friends, growing up."

"Do you really think this'll *all be over?*" Eris couldn't help but ask. "It feels so hopeless."

"Hope is the only thing we have."

"My parents are *dead,*" Eris snapped, a bit too loud. His voice cut through the quiet, still air. "What is there left to hope for?"

"Your sister," Mr. Chase said. "Miri. The friends you have who aren't aboard this boat but may yet still be alive."

Eris squeezed his eyes shut, trying to stave off the burning tears threatening to slip free. He couldn't cry, not again.

Mr. Chase's hand found his shoulder. "Get some rest, kid."

Eris wished he could.

There was a young man who hadn't said a word since Eris boarded. He stared out at the water surrounding them with a bleak, distant expression. Today, though, he spoke.

"Why are we doing this?"

"Doing what?" Miri's papa asked, frowning.

"Pretending things will be alright. Acting like we'll survive His Grace's wrath."

"Because we *will.*"

"Look around us. There is nothing. There will be nothing. I... I had a dream right before all of this. I'd drifted asleep in Einari's temple. He showed me what this world will be. Nothing but water. No life, no *humanity.* Why draw out our suffering? Why not end it swiftly? Wouldn't it be better that way?"

"No," Miri cut in. "It wouldn't be. Don't be rash. We'll find land again, and we'll be fine."

He shook his head. "I've seen it. There's nothing worth living for."

The conversation fell flat. Eris toyed with the fraying hem of his tee shirt. He picked at a loose thread.

When the man must have deemed nobody was watching, he stood, careful not to draw attention to himself. But Eris saw him, the way his gaze flitted to Miri's dads, to Miri, to the old lady and the young woman, then to Eris. He met Eris's eyes and held his stare.

Eris said nothing. He knew he should speak up. But the selfish side of Eris said, *if he dies, there's more drinking water for the rest of us.* Two half-gallon bottles, tucked beneath the seats near the bow. Only two.

This man seemed beyond convincing, anyhow, and Eris had little empathy to spare after being torn from his parents, forced to face the fact that they're long dead. He said nothing, did nothing, as the man dove off the boat.

He hit the water with a splash. Miri's dads gasped, scrambling to the boat's edge. Rob reached into the water, grasping for the man. But the man was gone. He had swam deeper than anyone could reach, unwilling to let himself be saved.

The lady who owned the boat cut the engine. They lingered nearby in case he resurfaced. He never did.

Eris had never learned the guy's name. He did not ask anybody. No point in learning the name of a dead man. Miri's dads closed their eyes and prayed for him.

Who will be next? Eris wondered. He glanced at Aria. Even if they somehow survived, how would she ever recover? Trauma at such a young age would bake itself into her psyche for the remainder of her life.

Eris did not have to wait long to find the answer to his question. When evening fell, the lady who owned the boat complained of an ache in her jaw. She was light-headed and tired, she'd said.

The strain of watching a man kill himself must have been too much for her to bear.

"Anders." Rob turned to Miri's papa. "You're near the storage compartment. Is there a blanket in there? Let's get her comfortable."

Anders peeked under his seat. "Nothing."

A blanket wouldn't have mattered, because in minutes, her breathing stilled, and her body went limp. She slumped against the tiller, her body weight turning the boat so sharp that everyone aboard lurched. Eris scrambled for the stern. He was the closest. With gritted teeth, he heaved the lady's body overboard before he could allow himself to think much of it.

Her name was Julie. Eris wished he didn't know. He knew everyone else's names. Miri. Aria. The woman in a crisp business suit, Celia, who had on occasion come by to ask Mom and Dad if she could borrow some flour or sugar or table salt. Miri's dads, Anders, Rob. Knowing their names would make watching them die hurt more.

With six people left, Eris now had space to claim a seat of his own. He helped Aria into one, then slumped into the seat beside her. Her eyes were glassy, distant, so wet they reflected the churning ocean. She clung to him as though he was the only thing keeping the boat afloat. Eris stared at her. She was the only family he had left. Eris squeezed his eyes shut, trying to fend off the flashes of Mom and Dad pressing her into his arms. *You're everything to us.*

He couldn't cry. Not again. He shoved Aria away from him and hugged his knees to his chest, forcing his attention away.

Celia sat with tall posture, her hands clasped. Her gaze darted between Eris, Aria, and Miri. "Please, Einari," she said, making no effort to keep her prayer quiet. A strand of curly brown hair fell from its tight ponytail and landed in front of her face. "Let the kids make it through this."

I should pray, too, Eris thought, though he couldn't stomach it. Einari was too angry to listen. And Aeris probably hated him, just as he hated Aeris. The only reason to pray to the god of the sky was in his parents' honor, which Eris was trying his hardest not to do.

The burden of grief was too heavy to bear.

Eris stood atop the ocean. The water was firm under his feet, though it splashed his ankles and drenched his socks. There was no boat, no buildings, no land as far as he could see—just flat water meeting a drab gray horizon.

Movement caught his attention, and he turned. He found himself standing before a familiar face, one with chiseled, pristine features and a long waterfall of hair, which turned to mist at his shoulders. His skin was blue, not tan, and he wore robes of a deep oceanic hue, hemmed with white lace, like sea foam.

Einari's true form.

"Your Grace," Eris begged, dropping to his knees. "I know you had a tough time on Midir, but we're not evil. We don't deserve this."

Einari's gaze was cold, unempathetic. Eris shivered as he stared up at the god looming over him.

"You stood by and watched that man kill me," Einari drawled. "And you did nothing."

"I—"

"Mortalkind, by nature, is a rotten thing. You will suffer. You will die. And when you pass the gates of Judgment, it is by my decree that you shall suffer more, Eris Vandermere."

Eris blinked. He stared up at the starry sky above, laying on his back upon the fishing boat's floor. His breaths came in short gasps, his lungs squeezing within his chest.

"Did you have a dream, too?" Miri asked, her voice soft, shaky. As he sat up, he spotted her, leaning against the boat's ledge, her chin resting upon her folded arms.

"He knows I lied about my name," Eris muttered. "He... He came to us. Personally. Out of the thousands of people he'd interacted with, he remembered *us*. I'd be honored, if his message wasn't so terrifying."

"We have to stay alive," Miri decreed, sitting up straight. She took Eris's hand and gave it a squeeze. "No matter what happens, we have to live. Out of spite."

"Out of spite," Eris repeated, cracking a halfhearted grin.

The water was rough and gray, as though a storm threatened the sea. But there were no storms here. No howling winds, no pelting rain. Only gentle, windless skies. The sky proclaimed, *"you will be okay,"* while the seas argued, *"no, you will die."*

Eris wasn't sure where to place his faith. How could he worship a god who had targeted him? Why pray to a god who saw him as a threat? But he couldn't worship the Fool, either, for the god of the sky offered nothing to save him from Einari's rage.

He turned to the goddess of the wilds.

Novika, hear me. Let us find land to take refuge on. Give us somewhere to rest, somewhere to find food.

Then, the goddess of fire.

Elaine, I beg you. Novika, Aeris, and Einari will not listen. Give us a small, contained flame, so we may cook fish. We are starving.

Eris gathered driftwood. He lined it up at the bow, where it might dry out with time. If they were lucky, it could serve as kindling.

Eris and Miri must have become a bastion of bad luck, though. Furious as the ocean was, with its choppy waves that spilled aboard, the wood slipped off the bow and splashed back into the ocean. Too keen on scooping water out of the boat with their hands, nobody paid any mind to the loss until the wood had long since washed away.

Eris was drenched in sweat. With every handful of water tossed away, another wave hit the boat, replenishing what everyone had worked hard to remove. Aria was of no help. She sat upon one of the seats near the stern, Mr. Squiggles in her lap, watching.

Frustration mounted. A six-year-old's hands did not hold much water, but she could have at least *tried.* Eris gritted his teeth and tried to ignore her. He scooped more water into his hands.

Hopelessly underprepared. That's what they were. Not even a single bucket. Still, Eris fought on, scooping water until his arms shook. *Out of spite.*

A fish flopped around in the boat. A gift from Einari? No, not likely. A handy coincidence. Exhausted, the boat's six occupants stared at the fish. Eventually, it fell still.

"I'm hungry," Aria warbled.

Eris balled his hands into fists. "We're *all* hungry! You're not special!"

"Eris," Miri's papa chided. His voice was soft. Gentle. When Dad used to get after him, he was firm, snappy. Eris wasn't sure which was worse.

Eris sighed, slumping into a seat. He wiped his damp palms on the fabric of his jeans, though his clothes were too soaked to help much. "She didn't even help."

"She's a child."

Celia dug through her business suit's pockets until she found a lighter and a pack of cigarettes. She lit a smoke and tucked it between her lips, then picked up the fish and flicked on the lighter again. The pitiful flame licked the fish's scales.

"That's not going to cook the fish," Miri said. She sounded defeated.

"Worth it to at least try, though, right?" replied Celia, her words garbled by the cigarette she held in her teeth.

Thirty minutes later, Celia's lighter ran out of fluid. The fish was charred in spots, uncooked in others. A waste.

"We need to eat *something,*" Miri's dad mused. 'Aria'll starve before the rest of us. We should get something in her, at the very least. Keep her alive."

Something horrid struck the back of Eris's brain. *Maybe we should let her die. It'd be more merciful, wouldn't it?*

No. No, he wouldn't dare sanction his little sister's death. The mere thought made him sick to his stomach, regardless of how frustrated he'd been with her today. She was more innocent than anyone else here. *I'll get her through this. Out of spite.*

"What about seaweed?" Eris asked. "We could try to dry some out."

"We lost our firewood trying to dry it out," Celia grumbled. Eris gagged at the acrid stench of cigarette smoke pouring from her lips. His lungs seized. His inhaler sat on his desk, somewhere at the bottom of the sea. "Best to just eat it wet."

Eris focused on digging seaweed from the ocean for the remainder of the day. By nightfall, he'd amassed a decent pile. Enough for everybody to eat. Enough to survive another night.

Sleep did not come easy. When he slept, nightmares plagued him. Images of Mom and Dad drowning, reminders of Einari's fury. *You are a monster,* Einari's voice echoed through his subconscious mind. *Irredeemable and corrupt, just like the rest of humankind.*

In the intermittent periods between bouts of fitful sleep, he tossed and turned, until eventually he gave up on sleep altogether, opting instead to stare at the blanket of stars above.

"We're running low on gasoline," Eris heard a low voice say. Rob.

"We'll use it sparingly," replied Anders. "Not like we're going anywhere, really."

Eris pretended he was asleep. He rolled onto his side, facing away from them. Their conversation faltered for a fleeting moment, as though they were worried Eris may have awakened. He took a deep, relaxed breath, the kind of breath one took when deep in the throes of slumber, and hoped he was convincing enough.

"We're low on fresh water, too," Rob said. "We're not going to last much longer."

Anders did not reply right away. Eris was not accustomed to the silence that night now offered. In the past, street noise and chirping bugs filled the gaps. Now, nothing. Not even the hum of the fishing boat's engine.

"Don't tell the kids," Anders eventually said. "Let them hope."

"They're smart. They'll find out."

"I haven't once seen Aria smile. And Eris... I wish I could've met him before all this. I wish I could've seen him when he still had light in his eyes."

Eris squeezed his eyes shut and prayed to the god of sleep. This minor god, unlike any of the Big Four gods, listened to his plea.

8

66th Dew, Prosperity 2192

"See that building over there?" Celia asked, pointing toward a skyscraper whose top floor, punctuated by tall, slender antennas, poked out above sea level. "There might be a few supplies in it. I'll swim over and take a look."

"Are you sure that's a good idea?" Miri's papa replied. "Could be dangerous."

"Any less dangerous than floating around in a fishing boat? I doubt it."

"We'll take you in a little closer, then."

Rob, stationed at the tiller, steered toward the building. The boat approached slowly. Rob was being gentle on the gas.

"Here," Eris chimed in when they reached a row of windows, pulling his phone from his pocket. He hadn't checked to see if it even worked. "This place looks like it still has power. If you get a chance, can you try to charge my phone?"

"Sure thing," Celia said. She smashed the window with a driftwood scrap, which she then tossed aboard the boat. She climbed inside. A shard of broken glass, still affixed to the windowpane, sliced through her leg, tearing her pants and drawing blood She winced, glanced at her leg, then carried on, disappearing into the building.

She did not return.

Not once did she stop by the window to give an update on her search for supplies. She never returned Eris's phone. She simply disappeared.

"Should one of us go find her?" Eris asked, sick of sitting around. He eyed the broken window. When Celia had smashed it, the water level was a hair below the windowsill. Now, water poured in.

"No," Rob's voice was firm and left no room for debate. "It's too dangerous. I hate to say it, but..."

"She's dead," Miri muttered when Rob trailed off. "And the best we can do is leave her, so we don't get hurt, too."

Electrocuted, maybe. Eris shuddered.

Rob said nothing more as he fired up the boat's engine and steered them away from the building. They lingered nearby, just in case. They all watched as the water level rose, as the rooftop electrical generator sparked, sputtered, and died.

That evening, a rowboat paddled by, packed so full of people that it risked sinking. They rowed parallel to the fishing boat.

"Do you have any water?" One man, who sat at the bow on his own comfy seat while seven others huddled in the middle, asked. He must have declared himself captain.

"None that we can share," replied Anders, shooting the occupants of the rowboat a kind, pitying smile. Eris knew what that meant. A discreet way of saying they were almost out without alarming him, Miri, or Aria.

"But you *have* some, though," the man pressed. His brows were low, tense, wrinkling the skin above the bridge of his nose.

Eris glanced over at Anders. His shoulders were tense, but he sat with tall posture, hoping to make himself more imposing. Eris figured if he were in the rowboat, he'd be plenty intimidated.

"What we have or don't have is none of your concern," Anders said. "I'm sorry."

The rowboat's self-proclaimed captain scoffed. He drew a small pistol and leveled it at Anders. "I'd think twice about that. Hand over your water or say your goodbyes."

Fast death or slow death, Eris thought. *Not much of a choice.*

Their remaining bottle of water sat under Rob's seat. There was not much left in it. A fraction. Not enough to sustain anyone for long. Anders frowned, narrowing his eyes in a thoughtful, calculative manner.

But in taking the time to come up with a diplomatic solution, Anders was not quick enough to respond.

An ear-shattering bang cut through the air. Anders slumped in his seat. He hadn't even had the chance to scream. Blood dripped from a bullet hole between his eyes.

"PAPA!" Miri screamed. Aria screamed, too.

Eris fired up the boat's engine and threw as much power as he could into it, sending the boat skidding across the waves, careening away from the rowboat.

The fuel gauge teetered near empty. *Please, be enough. Please, be enough. Please. I don't know if there's a god of gasoline, but if there is, help us.*

The man in the rowboat fired after them. A few bullets sailed over their heads.

And then, silence.

Eris sailed until the gas ran out. They were sitting ducks, now, and all Eris could do was hope they were far enough that the rowers would not follow.

Miri sobbed, slumped against Anders's knee. Rob pulled Miri into a tight hug. Not a consoling hug, but a needy one. Eris forced his gaze away. They deserved privacy. Aria, however, stared. Tears stained her cheeks. The kid was no stranger to death now, but this was the most gruesome, the bloodiest she'd seen.

Miri and Rob put together a makeshift funeral for Anders. They laid him upon the fishing boat's seats and, between hiccups and sniffles, prayed for his safe passage through Judgment. Eris found a few petals and leaves from some long-drowned flower floating on the ocean's surface, and he scooped them up and placed them atop Anders's forehead, concealing the bullet wound as best he could.

Miri gave him an acknowledging nod.

After prayer, Eris helped Rob and Miri carry Anders's body over the boat's ledge. The water swallowed him, taking him into its cold, choppy embrace. Miri and Rob lingered, staring at the water below, until Anders was long gone from sight.

"We'll get through this," Rob said, his voice thick with mucus and grief. He stared at his feet. How could he say that so soon after losing his husband? Was the pain not already enough to endure? Did he really have to lie, too?

"No, we won't," Eris snapped. "We're all dying. One by one. The gods are hunting us for sport. We're not going to *get through this.*"

Rob said nothing. He didn't even try to argue. There was no argument worth making.

Eris's gaze settled on Aria, her little hands squeezing Mr. Squiggles as though the stuffed bear were her lifeline. Maybe it was. Eris hadn't offered her much support lately. Or ever. His once-lively little sister was a haunted girl, now.

He owed her one final mercy.

9

67th Dew, Prosperity 2192

Eris triple-checked that Miri, Rob, and Aria were fast asleep. He waved his hand in front of their faces. He whispered their names. When nobody stirred, Eris closed his eyes and steadied himself. This wasn't going to be easy, nor pleasant. Not that either of those were plausible, these days. But this was for the best. The sooner he got this over with, the better. Right?

Eris scooped Aria into his arms as tenderly as he could. He pressed a little kiss to her forehead. "I love you," he whispered, his voice no more than a ghost of breath. "I'm sorry."

Then, in one swift motion, he plunged her headfirst underwater. She awoke the moment the frigid water hit her skin, and she thrashed in his grip. But Eris was bigger. Stronger. He held her firm, tears streaming down his face, and prayed.

Death, please be kind to her.

Aria used to run up and down the hall, pretending she was riding a horse. Eris, at the time, had put headphones over his ears and tried his best to tune out the thundering of little feet, the occasional *"Giddy-up!"* Now, he wished he'd appreciated her more.

I don't know what Einari told you to do, but I beg you to send her to Paradise. She's a child. She's done nothing wrong.

She used to tell Mom and Dad she wanted to be an explorer when she grew up. She refused to let her wispy blonde hair grow longer than shoulder-length—she insisted it would fit better into an explorer's hat, that way. "I'll be the first person to discover Era of Fire treasure," she'd proclaim, and nobody had the heart to tell her it had already been done.

Do whatever you want to me. Just don't bring her harm. I beg you. I'll do anything. I'll endure an eternity of torture if it means she gets a nice afterlife.

Bubbles streamed to the water's surface. Aria's thrashing grew weaker. Eris loosened his grip. Had he made a mistake? He didn't *want* his sister dead; it simply seemed like the most merciful option. Maybe he should stop, maybe he should save her. He still had time.

But then she'd know, wouldn't she? Wouldn't that be worse? He couldn't let her see who'd tried to kill her. He couldn't stomach the thought of looking her in the eye after this. He forced himself to hold her deeper beneath the waves.

"I'm sorry," Eris gasped. "I'm sorry, Aria, I'm sorry."

She stilled. Eris chewed on his lower lip. The taste of iron stung the tip of his tongue. He held her a few moments longer, then released her, and left her to sink.

When her body was gone, Eris clutched Mr. Squiggles close to his chest and sobbed.

Rob awoke first, come morning. Eris was curled up near the stern. His breaths came unsteady, unreliable, not filling his lungs the way they should. Rob joined him, pulling him into a warm hug.

"What happened?" Rob dared to ask. He did not mention Aria by name. Eris was glad he didn't. He wasn't sure he could bear it.

"She—she fell overboard," Eris managed to choke out. "I couldn't save her in time."

"I'm sorry."

Guilt and regret formed a nasty, blackened hole between his ribs, swirling, threatening to consume him. *Killer,* it whispered. *Liar. Sinner.*

Rob pressed the bottle of water into Eris's trembling hands. Eris stared at it.

"This is all we have left," Eris observed. "Enough for a couple sips."

Rob sighed. He opened his mouth, ready to concoct some half-baked lie, but he must have given up, because he said nothing of the sort. He averted his gaze. "...Yes."

"Have you had anything to drink lately?" Eris asked. "Don't lie to me."

"No. I've been saving it for you two."

"How long has it been?"

"Since I lost him." Rob muttered. He paused. "Please, don't tell Miri."

"Don't tell me what?" Miri asked. Eris had not noticed she'd awoken, but she was sitting on the deck with a firm frown, one elbow resting on the pad of Celia's old seat.

Eris said nothing. His gaze flitted over to Rob. *Tell her,* he urged. *She deserves to know.*

"We're low on water," Rob said. He gestured to the bottle in Eris's hands. "This is our last."

Miri's lip quivered. "Why didn't you say so? If we'd rationed it, it could have lasted longer—"

"We did ration it. Me, Anders, and Celia. But you, my priority has *always* been you."

"That's not an excuse!" Miri yelled. "I get keeping it from Aria, but from *us?* Did you really think we were incapable of handling it!?"

"Miri, take a breath."

"Those people. In the rowboat. They were willing to do *anything* for water. What do you think is going to happen to us? How much better will we be than them?"

"Einari must be laughing on his throne," Eris muttered, turning his gaze out to the ocean. "Flooding Midir with seawater. So abundant, yet undrinkable."

"Wait." Miri glanced around, and Eris's heart squeezed, sinking hot and low in his chest. "Where's Aria?"

Eris hoped the silence said enough. He stared at his feet, not eager to confront Miri's pitying stare.

He had once told Aria he would teach her how to play lacrosse. An empty promise, just to get her to stop nagging him about it. That day, she'd stood on the sidelines at one of his games, cheering so loud it distracted him.

When Eris had joined his family at the sidelines afterwards, downing his entire water bottle in a few gulps, she'd asked, *"Can you teach me?"*

At the volatile age of four, she'd taken to copying everything Eris did. She'd always wanted to be in the same room as him, and she had her heart set on lacrosse. Eris didn't want any part in it. *"Someday,"* he replied, placating.

Eris had found her propensity to copy him annoying. But she'd only ever looked up to her older brother. She'd stared at him with such bright, glittering eyes. Eyes that proclaimed, *when I'm older, I want to be like him.* And Eris, deep in the throes of middle school, had pushed her away. She was the new sibling, the thorn in his side, who'd revoked his status as Mom and Dad's only child. Mom and Dad bent to Aria's will. A luxury Eris never had.

Eris could not shake the image of Aria thrashing beneath the waves, her attempts to breathe air in vain. The way she had gone so still, her hair drifting with the current. Eris could still feel the back of her neck against his hand, so warm, her pulse thrumming against his fingertips.

And he had killed her. His own *sister.*

"Look at you," Einari sneered. Eris stood upon the ocean again, though now the water was deep enough to lap at his knees. Einari had not shown his face. His voice came from all around Eris. "Even you, who considered yourself so free of sin, are a monster. Don't you see? Humankind was a failed experiment."

Seafoam green eyes blinked open over the horizon like two moons, and Eris realized the blue hue of the sky was that of Einari's skin. He was massive, as though he held Midir in his palm, and he stared down into it like one would stare into a snow globe or a crystal ball. Eris was an ant to a god like him, waiting to be crushed under his divine boot.

Eris stared up at him with an odd mix of awe and fear. "Your Grace, I—"

"I care not for your excuses. You claim humanity is not evil, and then you contradict yourself? I can feel the shame rising within you. Good. Be ashamed. You are worse than any other. You may try to live— oh, what was it... 'out of spite'—but the moment you succumb, you will be sent to the darkest pits of Punishment. Now, I'm a merciful sort. If you see fit to beg, perhaps I could be persuaded to let you endure an eternity of rot instead of an eternity of torture."

Eris wanted nothing more than to grovel for forgiveness. But no matter how hard he tried, he could not move his limbs. He could not drop to his knees; he could not open his mouth. By the time he managed to curl his pinky finger, Einari was gone, and Eris's dream faded into nothingness.

Eris took a tiny sip from the water bottle, then passed it to Miri. She did the same, drinking only enough to wet her tongue, then handed the bottle to her dad.

Rob eyed the bottle with a longing thirst, but he screwed the lid on and tucked it away in its usual spot beneath the frontmost seat. Miri stared at him, her eyes narrowed.

"You're not drinking," she said. A statement, not a question.

"I'm not thirsty."

"Dad, don't."

Rob sighed. He brushed his fingers over his bald head, as though to comb them through hair that didn't exist. His darting eyes betrayed his defeat. "I'm saving it for you two."

Miri's posture slumped. Eris wasn't sure she'd ever looked quite this tired. Darkness rimmed the undersides of her eyes, barely concealed by her round glasses. Her skin was pale, though reddened in spots from the sun.

Somewhere on his phone, dead and lost beneath the waves, was a photo he and Miri had taken together, back when they still had reason to hope for their future. Miri had a bright, toothy smile, so wide her eyes squinted, the sage green of her irises obscured. Miri was a whole different person, back then, with dreams of going to conferences and graduating high school a year early.

Now, her brown hair was a mess. Unbrushed, tangled, damaged by saltwater. Her hair no longer framed her face in a charming, dare Eris say *cute* way, but rather, it accentuated her thinness, her drooping eyelids.

"What good will that do?" Miri asked, her voice breathy. "Aside from ensuring you die first?"

"It will sustain you long enough to find more supplies. Long enough to keep you going."

"That's not going to happen."

"Keep your head up, Miri. You won't find refuge if you don't fight for it."

Miri nodded, solemn. She spent the rest of the day sitting beside her dad, soaking up the last remaining fragments of time she had with him.

Eris gave them space. To busy himself, he found a chunk of driftwood and attempted to paddle the boat. His attempt was fruitless. His arms burned, and the boat moved no farther than it would have naturally moved with the waves. Eris didn't have anywhere to paddle *to,* anyhow. No distant land to strive for, no buildings to stand upon. Paddling was nothing more than busywork.

Rob grew lethargic and distant as the day passed. Miri kept offering him sips of what little was left of the water. He refused, even as the confusion and brain fog set in.

"I want to force the rest of our water down his throat," Miri admitted to Eris one evening. "But what good would that do but prolong his death and shorten ours?"

That was all it came down to, now. A matter of who went first.

Distant rain pattered against the sea. The first rain since the flood. Maybe the god of the sky would bring them mercy and kill them fast.

No. Aeris couldn't even do *that* right.

Eris and Miri watched the rain sweep across the ocean. By the time it reached the fishing boat, it had petered out, not much more than a trickle. Eris scrambled for the water bottle, uncapping it and leaving it atop a seat. If they were lucky, they'd catch a few drops of water.

When the rain stopped, Miri's dad drew his last breath. It came as a small gasp, a shudder, then silence.

10

Miri and Eris sat at opposite ends of the fishing boat. Miri perched at the bow, and Eris, at the stern. Neither exchanged a word. Not since they sent Rob's body below the waves. Not since Miri said with a broken, small voice, "He's with Papa now."

No gasoline. No water. No food. When was the last time they'd seen the top of a building? Not since Celia died. There was nothing but sea and sky. An endless expanse of blue. If Eris were to dive out of the boat and swim straight down, where would he end up? Would he still be in Anesh? Or had they drifted somewhere past the city, into unknown territory?

He stared into the water. Fish flitted below, but there was no sign of human development as far as his eye could discern. Light did not reach deep enough to touch houses or roads.

The air felt thinner, too, he'd noticed. His breaths came quicker, his heart rate faster, like he'd hiked up a mountain and was now standing at the peak. His lungs struggled to keep pace. He yearned for his inhaler.

The clouds were gray. Wind whipped between him and Miri, threatening a storm. Rain wasn't unheard of during dew season, but weather like this was far more common later in the year. Aeris must be angry. But why? What had mortalkind done to anger the god of the sky? Einari had been stalked, exploited, murdered. Aeris endured nothing of the sort.

Eris glanced over at Miri. She sat curled up, hugging her knees, her back hunched. Should he console her? What would empty words be worth?

"I killed her," Eris blurted instead. He didn't have time to filter the thought before it reached her mouth. "Aria."

Miri's tired gaze settled on Eris. She didn't say a word. Did she think he was being metaphorical? Or did she think him hideous, just like Einari did? *I'm disgusting,* Eris thought. *I'm sinful.*

"I thought it would be better that way, you know?" he choked. The silence unnerved him, so he filled it with his own babbling. "I thought it would be merciful. But it haunts me, Miri. I'm just as evil as the man who started all of this. I can't keep it bottled up anymore. It's eating away at me."

Miri stared. Eris wasn't sure how to read her expression. Pain? Resignation? Pity? To busy himself, he set the water bottle out on the seat, its lid off. Rain was imminent. Maybe Rob had been right. Maybe his death had kept Miri and Eris alive long enough to gather more water.

"Say something," Eris begged her. "Please. Tell me I'm awful. Tell me I deserve every ounce of punishment Einari has threatened."

"I don't think you're evil," Miri said, her voice breathy. "I don't think any of us are."

Eris buried his face in his hands.

Rain came, starting with a trickle, growing firmer and steadier by the minute. Eris sat back in his seat and turned his face to the sky. He opened his mouth, letting rainwater wet his dry, scratchy throat. Grime rolled off his skin with each droplet that hit his forehead, his cheeks.

He had not bathed or washed his clothes in a week. Never would he take any of those tasks for granted again. Clothes fresh out of the dryer, clinging to his skin thanks to the static that lingered in the fabric—if he could go back in time, he'd happily kneel on the living room rug and fold his, Aria's, *and* Mom and Dad's clothing for the rest of his life.

When the rain pelted down in thick sheets, the ocean responded with its own rage. The waves grew choppy and gray, rocking the little fishing boat. Miri sat up straight. She glanced at Eris, then looked up at the dark, swirling clouds above. When a wave set the boat off balance, Miri and Eris jolted, fighting to keep themselves upright.

Seasickness swirled deep in Eris's core as he clung to the ledge for dear life. Eris forced the nausea back. He refused to let Einari humiliate him. Even though he knew Miri wouldn't care, he had standards for human dignity, and those standards involved *not* vomiting into the ocean.

The boat crashed against something below the waves. A mountain? A building? Whatever it was, it sat high enough in the water to slice through the boat's underbelly. The sharp, ear-shattering *crunch* of tearing metal snapped Eris and Miri to attention.

Eris leapt to his feet as the boat flooded. He scrambled to find something to plug the tear. All he found was a roll of duct tape, mostly used. Not enough to cover a gaping hole. He chucked the duct tape into the water and scrambled for the bow.

"Miri!" he shouted over the wind and rain. He reached his hand out to her, fingers splayed, palm up. "Take my hand!"

Miri hesitated. Her wet, fearful eyes were trained on Eris.

"I'm not letting us drift apart," Eris said. "No matter what happens, hold onto me. Okay?"

Miri nodded. She took Eris's hand. When the boat went down, Eris plunged into the water, his body seizing and shuddering as frigid water assaulted his nerves. Miri squeezed his hand so tight he lost feeling in his fingertips.

He would take that over losing Miri any day.

Was there a point to staying afloat? No. Succumbing to the ocean would be easier, quicker, less miserable. But one glance into Miri's eyes kept him afloat. *Fight to stay alive. Out of spite.*

They floated until the storm subsided and the sun peeked out from behind thick clouds. Eris's left arm grew sore from treading water, his right hand still clasped with Miri's. Miri was struggling, her movements sluggish, her mouth and nose barely above water. Her breaths came in short, frenzied, desperate gasps.

When she slipped under the first time, Eris pulled her back up. The second time, too. The third.

The fourth time the ocean tried to take her, when Eris pulled her back to the surface, she gasped, "I can't do this anymore. Let me go, Eris."

"No," Eris gasped, horror striking him. "No, no. Hang on, Miri. We'll be okay. Hang on just a little longer."

Miri loosened her grip, but Eris held her tight. She peeled his fingers away one by one. When they drifted apart, Miri cast Eris a broken smile.

"You're the best thing that's ever happened to me," Miri whispered.

When Miri sank below the waves, Eris dove after her, desperate to grab her and bring her back. *Don't leave me. Please.* But he met Miri's soft green eyes, gentle, accepting of death, and he stilled before his hand met her skin.

Mercy.

Eris watched her sink. He watched the last bubbles of air escape her lungs. He watched her eyes drift shut as she sank further, further, until she was gone. Eris resurfaced with a gasp.

Miri had accepted death, as had Rob, as had the man whose name Eris never knew. They'd welcomed it. But Eris wanted to make a life for himself. He wanted to go to college on a sports sponsorship. If he kept treading water a little while longer, he could.

He bobbed along with the ocean's choppy waves for what felt like hours, even if it wasn't truly so. Maybe it had only been a few minutes. Eventually, though, the little voice in the back of his head—the voice of shame—made itself known.

Who am I kidding? I don't deserve to live. And even if I did, there would be no sports sponsorships left to accept. All the colleges are leagues below the water.

A slat of driftwood floated by, large enough to rest on. It taunted him from a reachable distance. But he didn't move. He couldn't bring himself to. It bobbed along, and Eris let his only chance of survival float away. There was no life left to live. Not with Mom, Dad, and Aria gone.

Miri, gone.

He floated on his back and stared up at the sky above. Storm clouds parted to reveal a gentle, cheery blue. The hot sun scorched his already-burnt skin. Even now, in his last moments, Aeris had the gall to haunt him.

The ocean pulled him under. He watched the way sunlight rippled and sparkled against the water's surface, casting wavering pattens of light onto the flesh of his arms.

His lungs begged for air. *Just one breath,* the tightness in his chest exclaimed. His fingers twitched, the lack of oxygen setting his nerves alight. Adrenaline spiked his heart rate. *Swim up, get air,* his body begged him. *Swim, swim!*

Eris breathed out. A slow, steady stream of bubbles drifted to the surface. His body convulsed. Darkness swallowed him. Darkness in the water, darkness in the corners of his eyes. On instinct, he gasped, and water flooded his lungs. Eris choked.

He felt himself fade. Slowly, then all at once. His body tingled, then went numb, until nothing remained but heavy, motionless limbs within Einari's embrace.

"Hang on, Miri. We'll be okay. Hang on just a little longer."
—The Grand Catalogue of Last Words: Great Flood Era. Death #0,000,10,462. Drowned. This soul was sent to Punishment by Einari's decree.

Blood of the Gods

Preview

"I'm unsure of whom I weep for more: those who have died or those who have survived. I have seen both sides. All that exists is misery."

—The Grand Catalogue of Last Words: Great Flood Era. Death #6,032,008,519. Drowned and resuscitated. Five weeks later, drowned.

5th Storm, Great Flood 1058

Captain Jonah Morgan was damn tired of taking in strays. The logic was simple: a larger crew meant solving more problems, and solving more problems meant caring about more people. The more people he cared for, the more he'd someday watch die.

When his gunner cried from above deck, "There's someone in the water!" and the subsequent pattering of feet knocked dust loose from the ceiling, his first instinct was to groan. This song and dance repeated far too often for Jonah's liking. Still, he shoved aside his weathered map and stomped from the lonesome safety of his cabin. Best to get the ordeal over with.

His crew was a measly four, minuscule for a square-rigged frigate such as the *Vengeance* but more than enough for Jonah's taste. They huddled at the starboard hull. His first mate straddled the gunwale, one leather boot in the dinghy, the other firm upon deck. Her neck-length sandy brown hair caught the morning sun, casting unflattering shadows upon her round face.

"Don't bother," Jonah snapped.

Karina Thorne ignored him, heaving her other leg over the gunwale. *Typical.* The dinghy, suspended against the hull by old, fraying rope, settled under her weight. With the crank of a pulley, she lowered herself to the water.

Jonah peered over the edge. The person in question clung to a soggy chunk of driftwood, fighting to keep their eyes open. "They're good as dead," he observed. "Malnourished, pale. Let them drown. More merciful that way."

Karina shot him an unamused glance as the dinghy kissed the ocean's glassy surface. Trembling and weak, the person in the water reached out. They weren't close enough, and their sallow, seawater-slick fingers didn't catch Karina's. Having leaned their entire weight forward, they lost their grip on the driftwood and fell into the water with an insignificant splash.

Jonah figured that was that.

Karina had other ideas.

She dove in, not resurfacing until she had her most recent pity project in her arms. A raven-haired head lolled against her shoulder as she pulled them onto the dinghy. Their limp body was no more useful than a paperweight.

The moment Karina hauled the sailor aboard, the patchwork crew of the *Vengeance* crowded around to catch a glimpse. "Back up," she said. The crew obliged, save for one. The gunner.

Jonah opened his mouth, ready to bark at her to scram, but Karina beat him to it. "Faye, fetch some towels, will you? They're soaked to the bone, the poor thing."

Faye swooped below deck, the vibrant shock of her tangerine shirt vanishing behind thick wooden doors.

Jonah eyed his first mate. "I'm not taking in anyone new."

"They were going to drown," Karina argued.

He knelt, rolling the sailor onto their side, lest they choke on any lingering seawater in their throat. Their body was as limp and pliable as a fresh corpse. A soaking wet mop of wavy black hair obscured their slack face, their cheeks too pale and yellowed to be healthy.

"They were cast overboard, I'd wager."

When Faye returned with a heap of ratty, fraying towels, Karina took one and brushed it over the sailor's damp skin. Their slender form shivered despite the storm season warmth.

Fat drops of seawater rolled from Karina's temple to her chin. She made no effort to wipe it away. "Or their ship sank. Have some sympathy, Captain."

Jonah felt none. But Karina was as whale-headed and stubborn as she was compassionate, and Jonah had the sinking feeling she would not budge. He sighed, begrudging. "Fine, whatever. We'll keep them aboard until they recover, and then they're on their own."

"Seriously, Jonah?"

"Yes, *seriously*. I'm done taking stragglers in."

Jonah rose and stalked away. He descended the creaky stairs, electing to ignore Faye's muttered, "Drama queen."

The cabin deck sat one level below the main deck. Here, a long passageway stretched toward the bow, doors to the crew's private cabins lining the bulkheads. The lights along the walls buzzed, their fixtures faulty but not yet worth repairing. Jonah hesitated at the base of the stairwell, his gaze drifting to the lone door at the end. He gritted his teeth and retreated to his cabin before that door could haunt him.

He returned his attention to his map. Tracing routes was a crucial job this far north. The *Vengeance* could not cross the 50° latitude. Any farther into Anui waters, where the churning ocean threatened to freeze, they'd be treading into pirate territory.

Jonah's mind drifted to Karina's rescue. A sense of profound wrongness radiated from her cabin. He needed to get this person off his ship soon for his own sanity. Who had Karina brought aboard? A pirate? A thief? A beggar? Regardless of who they were, they did not belong. From the look of things, the Midnorthern hub was two days' travel west—he could leave them there. The *Vengeance* was running low on supplies, anyhow. What was the phrase the ancients used?

Two birds, one stone.

Jonah dug out a sheet of half-used paper, old notes and reminders scrawled upon it, from his desk's centermost drawer. As he pressed the nib of his fountain pen to the paper, a knock at his door jolted him. Ink splattered the page. *Great.* He wasn't going to get any work done today.

Karina opened the door. Jonah jotted down his list before she could interrupt him again. Gunpowder, cleaning supplies, food...

"I hung their shirt to dry." Her voice was firm, demanding attention, which, on principle, Jonah refused to give. He did not look up from his work as she approached. "I couldn't help but notice they were covered in scars."

"So, they've been in a few fights," he grumbled. "No surprise. This far north, they're no doubt a pirate."

"They weren't normal scars. They looked intentional."

"Surgical."

"Not surgical."

He glanced up. Karina's hazel eyes were soft with concern and curiosity. She wore dry clothes now, but her hair appeared two shades darker than usual, thanks to the dampness clinging to it.

"Come. I want a second opinion, and I *happen* to value yours."

Karina took Jonah by the arm and tugged him from his cabin. Her fingers squeezed his bicep. Karina's muscle was less apparent on her stocky build than on Jonah's sharp, dense physique, but she had no issue lugging him across the passageway, despite his struggles to break free. She released him at the door, and he rubbed his arm.

Karina's cabin was far too cluttered for Jonah's taste. He couldn't see a speck of floor—a light pink shag rug blanketed most of it, and where the rug ended, shelves, crates, and trunks lined the walls, piled full of useless crap. Jonah had long since given up on his attempts to mitigate her hoarding tendencies—as long as her collection didn't spill *out* of her cabin, it was fine. So far, Karina had adhered to his policy.

In front of a propped-open window, the sailor's sopping clothes hung to dry. Every time Jonah laid eyes on those damned windows, frustration boiled within him. She and Mouse, the ship's engineer, had gone behind his back a few years ago to renovate, and they'd knocked out part of the hull to install big, garish panes of glass. Their project compromised the hull's integrity.

Atop Karina's cot lay her rescue, bundled in yellow sheets. Jonah approached with caution. He pulled the sheets back. The skin on their flat chest was as pale as their androgynous face.

"Male, then," Jonah muttered.

"Don't make assumptions. Now, look here." Karina turned their right arm supine. Along the forearm were neat rows of parallel scars, almost scientific in their spacing and thickness.

Jonah frowned. "So, what? He's got self-harm scars." *I've got plenty, too.*

"In any other case, I'd agree, but I'm inclined otherwise. Look—see this, in the crook of their elbow?"

Jonah leaned in and narrowed his eyes. There sat a tiny, round scar right where one would find a vein, almost unnoticeable.

"A puncture site," Jonah muttered. "To leave a scar, it'd have to be a frequent offense."

"Whoever they are," Karina said with a frown, "someone's been drawing their blood."

About the Author

Wren L. Rivers (they/them) is a transmasculine and neurodivergent author born and raised in Virginia. They are a jack-of-all-trades type creative. Alongside writing, Wren illustrates their own covers and character art. Everything Wren creates is 100% human-made and untouched by generative AI.

Wren prioritizes diversifying the fantasy genre with queer stories. *The Divine Archive*—a queer seafaring fantasy series—marks their authorial debut.

You can find Wren online at https://linktr.ee/corvidarcana.

www.ingramcontent.com/pod-product-compliance
Lightning Source LLC
Chambersburg PA
CBHW050418110726

47899CB00008B/2763